Half a World Away

Also by Cynthia Kadohata

Cracker!: The Best Dog in Vietnam
Kira-Kira
A Million Shades of Gray
Outside Beauty
The Thing About Luck
Weedflower

Half a World Away

CYNTHIA KADOHATA

Atheneum Books for Young Readers
NEW YORK LONDON TORONTO SYDNEY NEW DELHI

ATHENEUM BOOKS FOR YOUNG READERS
An imprint of Simon & Schuster Children's Publishing Division
1230 Avenue of the Americas
New York, New York 10020

For information about special discounts for bulk purchases, please contact Simon & Schuster Special Sales at 1-866-506-1949 or business@simonandschuster.com.
The Simon & Schuster Speakers Bureau can bring authors to your live event. For more information or to book an event, contact the Simon & Schuster Speakers Bureau at 1-866-248-3049 or visit our website at www.simonspeakers.com.
Book design by Mike Rosamilia; jacket design by Russell Gordon
The text for this book is set in Palatino LT.
Manufactured in the United States of America
First Edition
2 4 6 8 10 9 7 5 3 1
Library of Congress Cataloging-in-Publication Data
Kadohata, Cynthia.
Half a world away / Cynthia Kadohata. — First edition.
pages cm
Summary: Twelve-year-old Jaden, an emotionally damaged adopted boy fascinated by electricity, feels a connection to a small, weak toddler with special needs in Kazakhstan, where Jaden's family is trying to adopt a "normal" baby.
ISBN 978-1-4424-1275-0 (alk. paper)
ISBN 978-1-4424-1277-4 (eBook)
[1. Adoption—Fiction. 2. Intercountry adoption—Fiction.
3. Emotional problems—Fiction. 4. Abandoned children—Fiction.
5. Love—Fiction.] I. Title.
PZ7.K1166Ha 2014
[Fic]—dc23   2013031627

For George, forever and always

Half a World Away

Chapter One

J aden sat on the floor, holding on to a half loaf of unsliced bread. He switched his lamp on and off, the bedroom lighting up and darkening over and over. Electricity had always relaxed him. For sure it was the most amazing thing about America. He bit off the biggest chunk of bread that could fit in his mouth. It was sourdough, which he liked because it was so chewy.

On, off, on, off, on off on off onoffonoffon.

Thomas Edison had called electricity "a system of vibrations." Jaden loved Thomas Edison. Edison had more than a thousand US patents. He had invented things left and right. Jaden wouldn't hate life like he often did, if only he could invent that much.

He mostly wanted to invent anything related to electricity. Atoms were in constant motion, even when you were asleep. When you died, your personal electricity kind of turned off. And yet everything on the earth held constantly moving atoms. So even if your personal electricity died, your body still had a system of vibrations. Jaden hadn't figured it all out yet, but he would someday—he'd promised himself that.

He closed his eyes and stayed very still, concentrating on his electricity. He could feel a slight tingling in his hands. He hadn't even known what electricity was when he was first adopted from Romania four years earlier. In Romania he'd lived in four different group homes, and none of them had electricity.

Anyway, here he was at twelve, and now his adoptive so-called parents were adopting another child, a baby boy from Kazakhstan. He figured he knew why they were adopting again: They weren't satisfied with him. Whenever he thought that, he felt tears welling up. He didn't know if he was upset for himself, because they weren't satisfied with him, or for the baby, because if the baby was up for adoption, it meant the mother had abandoned him, and Jaden knew what *that* was like.

The baby's name was Bahytzhan. In his picture he appeared Central Asian, and he had scabs on his forehead—from bugs? That's how Jaden had gotten scabs on his face when he lived in Romania. Steve, his "dad," had made three copies of the Bahytzhan picture: one for himself, one for Penni, and one for Jaden. Jaden kept his copy in a drawer in his night table.

Off.

He sat in the dark. He could hear Penni calling him. He called her "Mom" to her face and "Penni" in his mind. He only had one mother, and she'd given him away when he was four. He could still remember her vaguely. But what he really remembered was the home where she'd placed him—twelve people, one room, one bed. He'd slept on the floor. And he remembered being afraid. When his mother left him, he'd been so out of his mind that he hadn't even screamed and cried; he'd howled. He could still remember the feeling when he'd howled, the feeling like someone was cutting through his skull and pulling out his brain, all while he was awake. Even today, sometimes he was in so much pain about it that he thought it would kill him. He did admit that this home in America was different and, yes, better than anywhere he'd lived in Romania. And yet he always came back to how Romania was his true home and how Penni and Steve had had no right to take him from there.

One of his psychologists had told him he should be grateful to Penni and Steve. The shrink didn't understand that they didn't adopt him for *him*, but for themselves. But what the guy really didn't understand was that it was impossible for Jaden to feel grateful, for anything ever. It wasn't personal to Penni and Steve. Jaden had a distaste for parents in general. And he knew he wasn't alone. There were hundreds, maybe thousands, of kids in America just like him—adopted when they were older, hating their new parents. He knew this because one of his psychologists or psychiatrists had said so. He couldn't remember at the moment which doctor it was. So he pretty much was nothing special.

"Knock, knock," Penni said from behind him.

He turned around, saw her shadow in the doorway. "I'm ready, Mom." They were going out to eat with Penni's older sister, Catherine, and her family. Things could have been worse for Jaden—he could have been adopted by Catherine: yuck. He let the bread slip from his fingers so Penni wouldn't see that he'd been eating before dinner.

He got up and followed her through the house. It was a nice enough house, but not *his* house. He didn't have a house. Never had—he'd only thought he had one. His mother, the only person he figured he'd ever loved, had given him up. He refused to feel love again, ever. Every day all he wanted to do was cry. He hated school, sitting there like a soldier in the army. He hated home, with Penni always trying to get through to him. He wished she would ignore him more.

Steve had just gotten home from work, so he was wearing a suit and tie. His suits were all slightly too small because he'd gained weight recently. "I hear you didn't go to school. Whatcha been up to all day?" Steve asked Jaden.

"Packing," Jaden lied.

Steve took off his wire glasses, cleaned them, and gazed at Jaden like he wanted to see him better. "It's unbelievable, isn't it? In forty-eight hours or so from now we'll be in Kazakhstan, meeting your baby brother." Steve smiled. Jaden looked at Steve's face. The smile looked real, not phony the way Steve's smiles sometimes looked. Steve used to be a smiling, lovable geek. But he'd changed. That is, Jaden had changed him.

"Yeah, cool," Jaden said.

It was raining, so the three of them sprinted out the door to the car.

Jaden always sat in the middle of the backseat, so that if someone came from one side and tried to pull him out to take him to a foster home—or wherever— he would have a better chance of getting away, out the other side. That was only a theory, of course, but he believed it. He saw Penni and Steve meet eyes, and then Steve started the car and said, "When we get Bahytzhan, we'll need to put the baby seat in the middle. That's where experts say it's safest."

Jaden didn't even answer. He couldn't sit on a side. Period. "I won't ride in the car anymore," he said. "I'll ride my bicycle everywhere." He felt bitterness well up inside himself, moving up from his stomach to his mouth, and he gagged slightly. He knew he was overreacting, but he couldn't help it.

Steve and Penni met eyes again. Penni turned all the way around. "Jaden, it's just that Steve read an article saying the baby seat should be in the middle. Okay?"

So this was all Steve's idea. Jaden didn't answer. He shook off the bitterness and stared out the side window at the rain falling hard on front lawns, at porch lamps lighting up the houses. It was hard to believe that this lit-up neighborhood existed on the same planet that he'd lived on before. If—*if*—he decided to go to college, he would study electricity, which he'd done a science project on at school. He'd hooked up a cocoon so that a tiny light would go on every time the future moth moved inside the cocoon. Then, when it was born, a bell would ring. He'd gotten his only A ever on that project. He didn't get an A for the class, though. He got a C. That was because the only thing that interested him was electricity.

Jaden knew it didn't make sense, but he felt like if his real mother could have had electricity, if she could have only plugged in a light and turned it on, she wouldn't have had to give him away. He'd told this to one of his former psychiatrists—a man whose name he couldn't remember—and the psychiatrist had asked, "Why do you think that, Jaden?"

"Because electricity is magic," he'd answered. That same psychiatrist was the first of many to say that Jaden couldn't attach properly to Steve and Penni because of being betrayed by the one caretaker he'd ever had—his mother. From age four to eight, he'd had to fend for himself in group homes.

"I kind of wish I hadn't let Catherine talk me into this dinner date," Penni was saying. "We've got so much to do before we leave."

"I too wish you hadn't let her talk you into it," Steve replied.

"I too" was exactly the kind of thing Steve said. "Perhaps" for "maybe," "distressed" for "upset," and so on. He was a word nerd.

Catherine was kind of strange because she was so different from Penni. Jaden had to admit that Penni was a nice person—he just didn't love her—but Catherine was less than nice. Much less. But Penni refused to see this because of "the importance of family." The importance of family was one of Penni's themes. Penni told him that the more family who loved him, the better. Jaden didn't even know for sure what anyone meant when they used the word "love." Was it like an electrical charge that developed between two people? He didn't know.

Chapter Two

It was just like Catherine to insist they have dinner together right before the big trip to Kazakhstan, when they were so busy. She said she had a big surprise for them. When they reached the restaurant, they got out of the car in a rush and hurried in, partly because of the rain and partly because Catherine and her husband, Marty, were very prompt people.

Sure enough, not only were Marty and Catherine already at the restaurant with their baby, but as soon as Catherine spotted them, she checked her watch. They must have been on time, because she and Marty smiled. Marty told everyone where to sit—Jaden between Catherine and Penni. "Jaden between the lovely ladies," was what Marty said, indicating a chair. Jaden sat down.

"Jaden, I swear you grow taller every time I see you," Catherine said.

"Yeah, I, uh, guess I'm growing."

"You certainly are! And I have to admit you're becoming a handsome young man."

"And he knows it!" Steve exclaimed.

Pride surged through Jaden. He *was* handsome. Whatever happened in the future, wherever he went, whatever he did, he had that.

Then there was a silence. Jaden hated these weird silences that happened sometimes at dinners. If you couldn't even be quiet without it feeling weird, why would you bother to have dinner together in the first place? In fact, this dinner proved just how *un*important family was. Finally he had to say something. Even though a shrink had told him not to speak impulsively, now Jaden said the first thing that came to mind. "The last time I saw you, all your baby did was cry."

Catherine and Marty put on their serious faces. "Well, she's a *baby*, Jaden," Marty said.

"Yeah, but she never laughs or smiles," Jaden answered, feeling a little defensive. The baby started to cry on cue. She was not a happy baby. Yet what would she have to be unhappy about?

"Well," said Penni. "Well. I'm famished." She glanced around for a server. "I'm going to order an iced tea. I need the caffeine, because believe it or not, I'm not even finished packing, and I need to wash and clean the money we're bringing. Did I tell you we have to take fourteen thousand dollars in perfect hundred-dollar bills? And my bank, who'd told me that they'd have the bills by today, ended up having exactly seven perfect bills? Seven?" Sometimes when Penni was trying to make peace, she said every sentence like it was a question.

"Have you communicated with your adoption agency lately?" Catherine asked. "I remember you saying they hadn't been answering your e-mails."

"I did hear from them, the other day. They're, um, well, they're going out of business."

"What?!"

"Yes, we were pretty shocked. But they say everything they needed to do for our adoption has been done. It shouldn't affect our process at all. Knock on wood."

"Knock on wood indeed," Steve said.

All the grown-ups started talking about the adoption and the agency, and also about how Jaden would have to "work at" being a good big brother. "But, ultimately, I'm sure he'll be a remarkable big brother," Penni said. She always stuck up for him, and Jaden knew she believed everything good she said about him. She believed good things that he didn't even believe himself. Though Jaden wasn't sure what love was, he was pretty sure that Penni felt it for him. The reason she'd sent him to so many psychologists and psychiatrists was to make him love her back. The one person he'd ever loved was his mother, who gave him away. So why love anyone? The shrinks hadn't worked, and Jaden ended up not loving anyone in the world. And then he started refusing to go to any more doctors. After trying to pry his hands off the bedpost in his room to take him to a psychologist, Penni and Steve finally decided not to send him to more doctors for a while. So right now Jaden was shrink-less.

"Why doesn't everybody decide what to order?" Marty said.

They all obediently picked up menus. Jaden's eyes went straight to the filet mignon Penni had promised would be there. Marty and Catherine were picking up the tab, according to Penni. So Jaden wasn't sure if he would be allowed to get two orders of filet mignon. His mouth began to water at the thought of nearly raw meat. He got only well-cooked or cured meat when he lived in Romania, because there were no refrigerators to keep meat from spoiling. "Can I get two entrées?" Jaden asked. No matter what he ate, he was always just so hungry.

"No," Marty responded crisply, not even lifting his head from his menu.

"Yes, you may," Steve said, also not lifting his head.

Then Steve and Marty raised their eyes at the same time. There was a pause. They both probably had something they wanted to say, but then they both pursed their lips and returned to their menus. Jaden felt a little guilty—sometimes he caused trouble even when he hadn't meant to.

Jaden decided on two orders of the filet mignon. He glanced at Penni because he could feel her eyes on him. She smiled. It was weird how he always knew when she was looking at him, like they were connected or something—even though he didn't *feel* connected to her.

She touched his hand, for no particular reason. His doctors always told him how much Penni loved him. Steve not as much, though the doctors never actually told him that. A couple of years back, when Jaden was starting fires in the house, Penni had refused to put him into residential treatment, even though Steve wanted to. Instead Penni had sent him to a psychiatrist, Dr. Wilder, who saw it as his mission to stop Jaden from starting fires.

Dr. Wilder actually read three books about electricity so he could talk to Jaden about it. He made Jaden go through behavior exercises every week. Like, once a day he was supposed to think of something good about Penni and Steve, and once a week he was supposed to tell them something good about themselves. Jaden didn't think that was why he stopped with the fires, but anyway, for whatever reason, he'd stopped. But then Dr. Wilder had given up his practice to write a book about relationships.

His next shrink tried to make him understand that setting fires was sometimes a behavior of kids who were adopted at older than four or five.

Jaden didn't understand why, and maybe nobody truly understood. Behavior, behavior, attachment, attachment. He heard those words over and over. When he thought of those other adopted kids setting fires all across the country, he wished that he could meet some of them, and not to start fires together. Just to talk.

Then his next shrink had tried to get to the bottom of why Jaden was so charming and cooperative sometimes and so utterly uncooperative other times. He thought Jaden might have a split personality. That was plain crazy. There was only one Jaden inside his head.

When the waiter appeared, everybody paused so Marty could decide who was going to order first, as was tradition on account of how bossy he was. Frankly, Jaden thought Marty could use a shrink himself.

"Jaden, why don't you order first?" Marty said.

Jaden felt a little electric jolt inside himself at the happy thought of ordering first. He cleared his throat. "I'll have two orders of filet mignon cooked rare." He held his breath, but nobody commented.

Jaden couldn't help smiling when the bread came. It was so beautiful. In Romania, the people living in his last group home would have scratched his eyes out for a slice of damp bread picked out of a garbage dump. He'd found bread twice, so he knew whereof he spoke . . . or whatever the phrase was. Now he took three slices of bread and six butters. The butter was perfect—not too hard and not too soft. And it was a little yellower than most butters. He loved that. He tried to spread it evenly over the whole slice. Buttering bread had to be one of the most enjoyable things to do in the world.

Steve said, "So how did your art project go? I forgot to ask you."

Jaden perked up. "Pretty good," he answered. "Mrs. Malady said it was my best art project this year." He'd cut and pasted bright pictures so that the final product looked like a stained-glass panel.

"Good for you. Bravo!" Steve said happily.

"I thought art was one of your weak subjects," Catherine commented.

That made Jaden want to mash butter in her face, but he rose above that. Penni said, "Our total travel time is thirty-one hours?" Everyone just stared at her for a moment.

"Can you believe I've never even been out of the country?" Catherine finally asked.

Actually, Catherine was so narrow-minded that Jaden could believe it, but he was good and didn't say so. He never got credit for all the times he was good.

Then everybody except Penni started ignoring Jaden and instead talking about adoption and work and vacations. Basically, they were talking about making money (work) and spending money (adoption and vacations). Penni was an administrative assistant, and her boss was letting her take three months off for the adoption. Seven weeks or more of that would be spent living in Kazakhstan. The reason the trip would take seven weeks was that Kazakh law involved seeing your baby two hours a day for two weeks in order for you and the baby to bond with each other. Then you had to wait (and sometimes wait some more) for a court date, followed by at least fifteen days when any of the baby's relatives or the prosecutor had the opportunity to protest the adoption. And then you had to do some paperwork. Often it all took even longer than seven weeks.

Anyway, since Jaden didn't have any money, none of this really concerned him. Penni would buy him whatever he needed.

When the waiter came with the food, Jaden watched with satisfaction. He took out his cell phone and snapped a picture of his plates, then put his phone away as everybody lifted their forks. He liked to take pictures of his life. Sometimes he didn't take a picture for a week, and then he took twenty the next day. He hoarded the pictures as if they were food. Sometimes he sat at his computer and studied the pictures, trying to find clues that would make his life make sense.

He ate as fast as he could. He noticed that Penni hardly ate anything, which meant more for him later. She knew how much he loved restaurant food. He felt a little blip of something, but he didn't think it was love. It was more like maybe he felt a really, really small bit of guilt over how easy it was for him to get things from Penni. In fact, he wondered whether it would actually make it harder for him to get things from her if he actually loved her. It was certainly something to think about.

After he'd eaten the entrées, Catherine wouldn't let Jaden get dessert because he'd already eaten too much, not that it was any of her business. Nobody else wanted dessert, so dinner ended pretty quickly. "Let me get the tip," Steve said. He put thirty dollars on the table.

Before everybody got up, Penni said to Catherine, "So what was the surprise?"

"I was saving the best for last—I'm pregnant!"

"Oh, congratulations!" Penni said happily. She got up to give her sister a hug.

"I hope you don't mind . . . I mean, you have to adopt and all."

Jaden figured that statement would be too much even for someone as nice as Penni.

"We *want* to adopt," Penni said coolly. Jaden was glad she hadn't let Catherine get away with a remark like that.

Catherine and Marty glanced at each other. Then Catherine said, "I have to say, Pen, that we're worried about your adoption agency. Have you considered that maybe you should start over with a different agency rather than paying more money on this adoption? You don't want to pay all your money and do all your paperwork, then go literally halfway around the world, only to have something go wrong and you would end up not getting the baby—if the child is even still a baby. What if the child isn't still a baby?"

Jaden was getting sick and tired of Catherine. He decided to stick up for Penni. "Mom has spent a lot of time thinking about this, and she feels they're doing the right thing. It's a little late for you to butt in."

Penni and Steve didn't say anything, but he could tell they were pleased he'd spoken up. Steve's mouth twitched into an almost-smile.

That shut Catherine up. They all pushed back their chairs. Jaden lingered until everyone's back was turned, and then he pocketed the thirty-dollar tip.

In the car all he could think about was Catherine's question, "What if the child isn't still a baby?" "Getting a baby" was an important issue. Nobody had said this, but Jaden knew that it was a lot easier to adopt a kid who wasn't a baby. A lot of countries, including the United States, had way too many older kids to give away. At eight years old, he hadn't been worth the spit on an envelope.

Chapter Three

Jaden liked to hoard food, which was another
issue. A psychiatrist had told him he hoarded
because he'd weighed only thirty-eight
pounds when he was eight. The first year he was in
America, Steve had given him plastic containers for
the food he stockpiled under his bed. But a therapist
had thought Jaden needed to "normalize." The therapist must have come from a really normal family
because she was very concerned with normalizing
Jaden. She suggested no television, no video games,
and no computer unless he stopped hoarding. But

nothing worked—Jaden had to do it. He had to, and then they changed therapists.

Another not-normal thing he did was that from the beginning, he slept on the floor almost every night, even though Penni had tried to persuade him to get into his bed. But often he just wanted to sleep on the ground. He liked the way it was familiar and safe to him, whereas the bed made him feel uneasy. Penni had suggested putting the mattress on the floor, but after they did that, he slept instead on the box spring. It was the hardness that appealed to him. So they'd put the mattress back on the bed.

Now, Jaden used a flashlight to search through his closet. The back of his closet was where he kept stuff he stole or was otherwise special. He used to steal in Romania, and he'd kept that up in America. That was probably one reason he'd continued getting transferred to different group homes in Romania. He stole food, money, and other people's photographs. The food and the money—anyone would want those. But the pictures were something else.

He'd never owned a single picture, and some of the kids had pictures of families. Once in a while he just had to have those, even if only to tear them up.

Jaden thought he heard someone and spun around, but the doorway was empty.

He reached into the back of the closet and picked up a pair of too-small canvas summer shoes he'd gotten when he first moved here. Inside each shoe were a few pieces of candy. He studied each piece and finally picked out a packet of three chocolate malt balls. Then he slipped the thirty dollars into one of the shoes.

Back at his lamp, he began switching it on and off, sucking on a malt ball, trying to make the candy last a long time in his mouth. It was one of his remaining pieces of candy that he'd gotten on his first Halloween, when he'd been in the United States for about two months.

He wished he could go back in time to that Halloween. He could still remember how incredibly, amazingly exciting it had been. He'd gotten three full bags of candy, and he'd hidden it all in his closet. He'd been scared that Penni and Steve would take it from him, even though they said it was all his. Even today, once in a while he ate a piece to help him remember that hopeful, happy night, when he thought everything would be okay here in America.

These days he got sweets from Penni once a day, so Halloween, while fun, wasn't as exciting as it had been that first time. He probably wouldn't even bother to go trick-or-treating this year. One of his shrinks had said his fixation on candy was like a much younger kid's. Shrinks had opinions on every little thing about you, even candy eating.

Jaden sat on his bed in the glow from his fancy night-light. A girl from school who had a crush on him had given him the night-light for Valentine's Day. It was kind of cool. It was based on a Frank Lloyd Wright design, because he'd mentioned Frank Lloyd Wright to the girl. Wright was a famous architect who'd designed a number of houses in the Chicago area. Last year, Penni had driven several hours to take him to see a couple of the houses. And he had to admit that they were amazing.

Penni felt that she needed to educate him on America. When he'd learned enough English, she showed him movies like *Forrest Gump*, *Titanic*, and *Rocky*. In music, she had him listen to the Beatles, though they weren't even American. He watched film clips of American girls screaming insanely and crying at a Beatles concert. He thought a long time about that, and finally he decided he understood why they cried that way. It was because happiness and pain were kind of the same thing. For instance, Penni loved him a lot, which made her really happy but also caused her a lot of pain because, well, because of the way he was: broken. Let's see one of his shrinks go through Jaden's life and come out normal on the other end.

"Knock, knock."

He turned on the light. "Hey, Mom." She handed him a container that he knew held the remnants of the pasta she'd ordered at dinner. "Thanks."

"You're very welcome."

She sat down cross-legged beside him, and he stiffened as she touched his cheek, then started to softly sing "What a Wonderful World." It wasn't just a song she liked, it was an anthem. That song meant less than nothing to him. The fact was, it wasn't a wonderful world, and no amount of singing and eating big meals was going to change that. Then, for a moment, he felt a total lack of respect for her.

Steve peered into the room. "Good night, you two—I'm going to bed. I've got to get up at four to do a bit of work at the office before we leave."

"Seriously? You're going to work tomorrow?" Penni asked.

"Got no choice. I just found out today that I'm finally getting a chance to talk to the people at the Cal-Mex restaurant chain, and I need to polish my presentation and then meet them early for breakfast."

Penni sighed but said, "Well, okay, good night, hon."

Steve lingered, and Jaden knew why.

"Good night, Dad."

Steve walked off. He was actually an okay guy. But Jaden had made him very, very tired over the years. Jaden noticed more and more that Steve needed a break from him. Steve bought a motorcycle that he rode every Sunday. That was the one thing he had in his life that was fun.

Jaden opened the container and picked up some pasta with a fork Penni had brought. The food was like energy filling him up—he could feel his electrons going crazy. Penni watched as he ate. Steve thought he'd be fat when he got older, but Penni always pointed out that somehow or other he was still below average in weight.

Penni sometimes got fascinated by watching him eat. He thought it made her feel good, really good, to see him enjoying something so much.

When he'd gulped down the pasta, Penni stood up. "Okay, get some sleep. I'm serious. We have a lot going on for the next few days. Don't forget to brush your teeth."

"Sure."

He watched her leave. Then he switched off the light and slid down to the floor on the side of the bed not facing the doorway. He didn't even pull his quilt off the bed. He had a handmade quilt that was supposed to be really special or something. He got up and opened the window, then lay back on the floor and listened to the rain pounding outside. The temperature was unseasonably cool, and the cool air whooshed and whooshed over him.

Chapter Four

It was still dark out when he opened his eyes. He sat up to check the clock: 4:10 a.m. He could hear Steve and Penni talking, but he couldn't hear what they were saying. He pushed himself up and walked into the living room. Penni and Steve were holding hands on the couch, their faces happy. "What is it, Jaden?" Penni asked.

Then he realized he didn't know why he'd gone into the living room. "I don't know," he said honestly.

"Honey-darling, come sit with us," Penni said.

Jaden hesitated, then sat on the other side of Penni. She smiled. "Are you packed?"

"Yeah, I'm done."

"Good." She paused, then smiled again. "Thank you for giving Catherine a piece of your mind."

Jaden half smiled back, and Steve chuckled and said, "How in heaven's sake did you end up the sister of such a pompous, obtuse, pretentious whatever she is? I think she's humanoid, but I'm not sure."

"She's good inside," Penni insisted.

"You think everybody—" both Jaden and Steve started at once. Jaden paused and Steve continued, "You think everybody is good inside."

"That's because everybody *is* good inside," she said. "Well, maybe not every single person."

"You're the only one who's good inside," Jaden said. "I'm not."

"Of course you are!" Penni exclaimed.

She had so much faith in him. Even after all the lies he'd told her—about setting fires and ditching school and stealing—she still had faith in him.

"What if you don't like the baby?" Jaden suddenly asked Penni. "What then?"

"Of course I'll like the baby."

"You didn't like *me* at first."

"Of course I did."

"Well, at first you did, and then you didn't."

"She most certainly did," Steve said. "Most certainly and indubitably."

"She got mad at me all the time."

"Oh, Jaden!" Penni cried out. "Even if I get mad at you, I still love you. And I wasn't mad. I was exasperated."

Jaden knew that there were lots of nights when she had cried in bed for hours because of him. He'd heard her. Then somehow Dr. Wilder had helped him out of the fire setting, and the way Jaden saw it, it was only then that Penni loved him wholeheartedly. He had heard Penni on the phone begging Dr. Wilder to keep seeing him while he was writing his book. But that hadn't worked out.

"I know," Jaden said, though he didn't know. He

went back to his room and lay on the floor again. His teeth chattered from the cold, but he didn't close the window, just lay there shivering. He refused to get warm. And he refused to love anybody or anything, including that quilt.

He heard laughing from the living room, which made him feel lonely, and then it grew quiet. Steve seemed to have left for work. Jaden closed his eyes and kind of fell asleep, and he was surprised to open his eyes and see Steve leaning over him saying, "Jaden, get off the floor."

Steve hadn't woken him up when he was on the floor ever since Dr. Wilder had told them to let him sleep down there if he preferred it.

"Hey, buddy, how'd you like to come to work with me today? See how the best salesman in the state wins over a new client." Steve was a salesman for a food distribution company. The company delivered food to restaurants and institutions. It was called Sherman Manufacturing and Distributing. SMD. Jaden loved it when Steve took him to work. It was in what Penni liked to call "a bad neighborhood." There were homeless people sleeping on the streets a block in any direction. They really interested him. Tall barbed-wire fences surrounded all three of the company's buildings.

"Today I'm trying to sell our frozen soups to the Cal-Mex chain," Steve said. "Wait, not 'trying,' I'm *going* to sell them our soups. They're one of the biggest Mexican restaurant chains in America."

"I like the frozen corn soup best," Jaden said. "I like the bits of corn because they taste so fresh. And I like the mushroom soup second best."

"It's the best corn soup on the market," Steve said proudly. His eyes went dreamy. Then: "Quality ingredients equal quality results."

"Cool."

Steve had probably been a happier man before Jaden came. Now Steve often was on guard, and there was something sad about him. At this point he definitely liked work more than home. Jaden imagined Steve got a thrill whenever he won over a new restaurant or hospital or school. The schools usually bought some of the lower-grade items, while some of the restaurants bought what the company used to call the "premium" line. Then SMD changed it so that the lowest-grade items were called "premium" and the highest-grade items were called "super-premium." They also added a line called "premium value-added," which was in between. Value-added had become their most popular line.

"Get up and get dressed, and we'll head out."

"No, absolutely not, he is not going with you," Penni said, appearing in the doorway. "It's too much stimulation. We're going to Kazakhstan today! You know what Dr. Morgan used to say about overstimulating him."

Steve asked, "Which one was Dr. Morgan?" But he got up and left the room, stopping to kiss Penni.

"Jaden, it's freezing in here," Penni said.

She worried too much about things. It was annoying. "I'm sleepy," Jaden said, which didn't have

anything to do with it being cold, but his sleepi-
ness was suddenly urgent. He needed an unusual
amount of sleep every night—like, twelve hours.
He closed his eyes and had a vague feeling that
Penni had shut the window, but he was already too
far gone to know if the room was warm or cold.

Chapter Five

Jaden opened his eyes. It was light out, and the quilt lay on top of him. He got up. Penni was standing with her hands on her hips over his suitcase. "You haven't even started packing," she said, shaking her head. "I believed you."

She'd opened his suitcase. "Really, I'm not packed?" Jaden asked. The way lying worked was, you couldn't back down even when it was obvious you were lying. "I thought I was packed."

"Pack it," she said. Then she left the room.

Jaden threw the quilt on the bed. There was

nothing in his suitcase except seven gifts. Penni and Steve were supposed to bring gifts to give to the baby house director, numerous baby house workers, the interpreter, the driver, the adoption facilitator in Kazakhstan, and so on. The more important the person, the nicer the gift. Penni had bought twenty-one gifts at various levels of expensiveness.

Penni, Steve, and Jaden each had to carry a third of the gifts in their suitcases. Jaden rummaged through the gifts he'd be carrying. There were cheap-looking makeup trays with ten different colors of eye shadow each, sunglasses from someone named Tory Burch, two bottles of whiskey that was called Johnnie Walker, and a fake orchid that he knew had cost two hundred dollars. It was Jaden's turn to shake his head. He tried to imagine them giving a fake orchid to someone at the last home in Romania he'd lived in. That would have been ridiculous.

He opened his sock drawer. It was late summer,

and it was hard to know exactly what the tempera-
tures would be like seven or more weeks from now
in Kyzylorda, the part of Kazakhstan they were
going to. He chose three pairs of thick socks and
three pairs of thin socks. If he wore each pair two
days in a row, the socks would last him twelve days.
Underwear—six pairs. Then he pulled open two
drawers at once: his sweaters. According to Steve,
Penni spent a fortune every year on his sweaters.
She had a thing about sweaters—she got them for
Steve, too. Jaden stared at them, then picked two
that happened to be on top and dropped them into
his suitcase. He closed the sweater drawers and
opened his hoodie drawer. He chose five hoodies
and threw them on top of the sweaters—hoodies
were the most essential part of his look. Then he
threw in three pairs of sweatpants, a few T-shirts,
two pairs of jeans, and one extra pair of shoes.

He also filled eleven Ziplocs with his favorite
granola from the kitchen and zipped them into his
suitcase. After that he sat on the bed with nothing

to do. Then his heart skipped a beat: He was feeling that strange tingly sensation he used to get when he wanted to start a fire. He took a few deep breaths and tried to concentrate on electricity, the way Dr. Wilder had taught him. Dr. Wilder said thinking about electricity was a positive and thinking about starting fires was a negative.

So. The Greeks had known about the existence of electricity since 600 BC.

Electricity flows freely through metals because metals have electrons that separate easily from their atoms.

What else? Jaden tapped his fingers over and over on the bed. Then he thought about sitting on a plane for more than twenty-four hours, not counting layovers, and that made him jump up and head for the front door.

He went outside to do what Dr. Wilder called his "aggressive running." The rain was still pouring. Jaden closed his eyes and leaned his head back, letting water wash over his face. Then he started to run as fast as he could around and around the house. It was hard to reach maximum speed because the ground was wet and slippery. When he felt he was running as fast as he could, he threw himself forward onto the wet ground.

Unhhh. A rock ripped into his palm. He stared at the slash of blood, at how bright it was. He sank into the wetness, resting his cheek in the cool mud. Lying there made him realize he was still sleepy, so he went back inside and lay down on the bed for once. He idly watched blood drip onto his quilt.

When he woke up, there was a white bandage around his hand, a spot of blood seeping through. It was hard to disturb him when he was sleeping, because when you'd lived with eleven other people, you could sleep through anything. He unrolled the bandage, each layer bloodier than the previous one, until finally he reached the rip in his palm. He studied it calmly. It was jagged and about two inches long but no longer bleeding. He tended to bleed a lot when hurt, so Penni had bought bandages that helped clot blood. She kept some at home, carried some around in her purse, and always made sure he had some in his backpack. He wrapped the bandage around his hand again.

He yawned and pushed himself up. There was blood and mud on the quilt. One o'clock—he'd been more tired than he realized. Their flight was at eight p.m., and they were leaving home at three. They lived two hours away from O'Hare Airport, but Penni and Steve wanted to get to the airport extra early.

The house was silent. "Mom?" Jaden called. Nobody answered. He walked through the house, but it was empty. He didn't see Steve and Penni's suitcases. Had they left for Kazakhstan without him?

Back in his bedroom, he checked his cell phone. There was a text from Penni: BE RIGHT BACK. BANK HAS FRESH 100S. Penni had been worried about those perfect hundred-dollar bills for weeks, because she and Steve wouldn't be able to adopt without them.

There was another text from the girl at school who

liked him. He wasn't sure if he liked her or not, but he'd given her his phone number. She'd texted, HAVE FUN IN KAZAKHSTAN!! SEE YOU WHEN YOU GET BACK!!!!! She was into exclamation points. He texted back, SURE, SEE YOU THEN.

Jaden opened up his suitcase again. Threw in an extra hoodie. He was supposed to bring the suit they'd bought him for when they went before the Kazakh judge to get their baby's adoption approved. But he didn't want to wear it. It looked stupid.

The front door opened, and Jaden heard Steve's heavy footsteps moving quickly through the house. "Sorry I'm late! Penni? Pen?" When nobody answered, Steve moved from room to room. Jaden could picture him, the way his feet turned out as he walked. When he reached Jaden's room, he paused. "Where did your mother go?"

"She found some crisp bills."

"Excellent! Say, what's that on your hand?"

"Uh, I hurt it."

Steve stared at him for a moment. "Are you okay?"

"Yeah, it was nothing."

Steve tapped his fingers against the door frame and cleared his throat. "I know we've been busy with the adoption, but if you ever want to talk to us or hang around with us, you know we're there for you, right?"

"Right," Jaden replied.

Steve paused. "So did you want to talk?"

"No. I tripped in the mud. I'm okay."

"Were you doing your aggressive running?"

"No."

Steve took a big, tired breath. Jaden knew how tired he made Steve and Penni. In fact, when he first got to America, they had a lot more energy.

"Okay," Steve said. "Okay." His eyes moved back to the bed. "You know, your mom paid six hundred dollars for that. It's a vintage Amish quilt."

Jaden didn't know what "vintage Amish" was, but seriously? Six hundred dollars? Jaden eyed the quilt as Steve came in and gathered it up. Six hundred for that? He didn't even know you could buy a blanket for that kind of money. He did know they'd bought him a lot of nice things before he got here, the same way they'd bought a lot of nice things for the baby's room.

Steve rushed away with the quilt.

Jaden went to stand at the window. It seemed like the hardest rain he'd ever seen, a legendary rain, the drops beating on the window as the wind blew harder. Hard rain always reminded him of something, but he could never remember what. It was something from long ago, before his mother gave him away. He stood at the window, staring, then took a picture. When he saw Penni pull into the driveway, he stepped away from the window and checked the clock. Two thirty. His heart sped up. A lot of things were going to change. He wondered whether Steve and Penni might give him away. Sometimes Americans did that when an adoption didn't work out. But he'd been with them for four years. Could they still give him away? He didn't know how that worked.

The front door opened, and Penni called out, "I got the bills! I got the bills!"

She and Steve talked excitedly. Jaden stepped back in front of the bedroom window. The rain was like a magnet for him. A fuzzy picture of his mother was trying to take shape in his head. But he couldn't quite see her.

Chapter Six

At the airport the security lady frisked Jaden because he was wearing a baggy hoodie and baggy pants. She made him empty his pockets, which were filled with bread. "Bread?" the lady said. "Why is there bread in your pockets?"

"Uhhh." Jaden thought a second while the woman glared at him. "In case I get hungry. . . ." He felt his face redden.

"He's not going to hijack a plane with bread," Steve said impatiently.

The lady gave Steve a withering look. "I'm just doing my job," she snapped at him.

When they were walking away, Jaden heard Steve mumble, "Nitwit." If there was one thing that Steve didn't like, it was nitwits.

As they sat waiting for the flight to Frankfurt, Penni and Steve kept giving each other meaningful gazes, sometimes smiling and sometimes not. Once in a while Penni would give Jaden a smile, and even kiss his hand.

And he felt it again, that thing that wasn't love. It was more just that he felt safe. But it wasn't unlimited. If he had really succeeded in burning down the house, even Penni probably would have been willing to send him away to wherever adopted kids like him got sent to. There were special homes.

They alternately wandered and sat for the next couple of hours. Once, after they'd been sitting in the same place for an hour, Steve pulled Penni up and they started waltzing through the rows of chairs. Jaden felt curious about—just really interested in—their happiness right then. They were bright, very bright, their electricity on full blast.

When boarding finally started, Steve stuck both his hands behind him, and Penni let him pull her forward. "You too, Jaden," Steve said.

Jaden took the hand stuck out at him as Steve pulled. Penni took Jaden's other hand and held it. He kept almost tripping, and he was glad when they all needed to let go as they entered the plane.

"I'll arm-wrestle you for the aisle," Steve said to Jaden.

"Me?" Jaden asked. "I want the window."

"Good, because I want to sit between my two favorite people in the world," Penni said happily.

They sat in the back row of the plane. They'd bought the tickets from a travel agency that specialized in international adoption, so the tickets were discounted and quite possibly the cheapest on the plane. After they got situated, Steve leaned over and kissed Penni with a big *mmmmm* noise. Yesterday that would have embarrassed Jaden, but now he watched curiously. Here, now, on this plane, what would have embarrassed him yesterday didn't matter. He was entering a new world, the way he'd entered a new world when he came to America.

The plane began shaking hard almost as soon as it took off, and Jaden worried that maybe they were doomed to die while on their way to adopt this baby. Occasionally the shakes were violent, bouncing Jaden hard against his seat belt. His heart sank, and it must have shown because Steve said, "Take big breaths and breathe out slowly. Don't worry, if there was a problem, the pilot would land. It's just normal turbulence."

"I can't stand it!" Jaden cried out, surprising himself. A couple of people twisted around to look at him, but he didn't care. He felt trapped in this plane. He wanted out—*now*.

"It's a bit much," Penni said. "I've never felt this

much turbulence before." Her forehead wrinkled with worry. "Maybe we should ask a flight attendant about it."

"They're probably all buckled in," Steve said. "Don't worry. The pilot wouldn't do anything unsafe. He wants to live."

"How do you know?" Jaden asked, but Steve didn't answer.

Jaden closed his eyes and tried taking big breaths and exhaling slowly. There. That worked a little. A big jolt shook the plane, and he squeezed his eyes tight. He opened his eyes and wrinkled his forehead at Penni, who put her arm around him.

"Don't worry," Penni said. "It's—uh—"

Another big jolt stopped her from talking. Jaden wished there were a way to take a photo of turbulence. He saw Penni's eyes grow scared. That worried him a lot. Then he heard another passenger crying. Jaden thought they were all going to die.

"Mom?" he said.

"Yes?"

"I stole the thirty-dollar tip Dad left on the table at the restaurant last night."

She blinked at him, and for a second he thought she was going to be angry.

"Oh, Jaden," was all she said at first. Then she squeezed his hand. "Thank you for your honesty. Now is not the time for me to be mad."

Steve said, "For crying out loud, you two, stop acting like somebody's on their deathbed."

Jaden said, "Dad?"

"What is it?"

But he couldn't think of anything he wanted to confess to Steve. "Never mind," he said.

"Read—my—lips, you two," Steve said loudly. "Everything—is—fine."

The PA crackled, and then a man started speaking. "This is your pilot, Captain Mattson. As you all can tell, we've encountered a bit of turbulence. As we reach altitude, the turbulence will settle down. In the meanwhile you all keep your seat belts fastened, and the flight attendants will begin serving drinks before you know it."

He sounded almost amused. Jaden tried to let that calm him down. He didn't want to die, because he wanted to see his biological mother again, just to ask her, *Why? Why did you give me away and keep your other son?* He couldn't think of a single explanation, not one, but maybe she had an explanation he hadn't thought of.

The plane rose through some clouds, so that Jaden couldn't see any city lights or anything down below, like they were suspended in nothingness. He stared out at the nothingness for hours, "turning off," as Dr. Wilder used to call it. At one point he could hear Penni say—as if from far away—"He's turned off." He stared outside. Once in a while he turned off for days. There was no predicting how long it might last.

Chapter Seven

He must have fallen asleep, because the flight attendant was announcing that they would be landing in Frankfurt and that everyone should raise their trays and bring their seat backs up. Relief flooded over Jaden, even though the shaking had resumed. When the pilot said, "Flight attendants, prepare for landing," a few people applauded.

Jaden smiled at Penni. He felt giddy that they were still alive. When the plane touched down, there was more applause. He briefly regretted telling Penni about the thirty dollars, but oh well.

Jaden never wanted to get on another plane again, but he knew that in a few hours they would have to catch their flight to Almaty, Kazakhstan. He wondered if it would be possible for him to stay in Frankfurt for a few weeks. "Hey, Mom, do I have to go to Kazakhstan? Can I stay here?"

"Jaden, of course you have to go to Kazakhstan. You can't stay in Germany by yourself. Plus, you need to bond with the baby before we come home. The bonding period is not just for the parents but the whole family."

"I hate flying, Mom."

"How can you hate flying? You've only flown twice."

"Both times were awful."

"That's it," Steve said. "No more talk about flying. Let's talk about the beautiful future. That's what matters now." Then Jaden knew what Steve was going to say before he said it. "A positive attitude equals a positive outcome."

"You're absolutely right," Penni declared, as if

that were the first time Steve had ever said that.

"But, Mom," Jaden said.

"Enough," Penni answered firmly.

The thought of more turbulence made Jaden feel like he was going to lose his mind. He gagged, but Steve and Penni didn't notice. He hoped it happened again while they were watching. Then maybe they would understand how upset he was about flying.

They strolled around the sprawling airport. On a whim Steve bought caviar and crackers at a food shop. Then they sat down, and Steve handed Penni a cracker topped with caviar. Penni said, "Mmmmmm," and closed her eyes. Jaden felt his mouth water, but when he stuck the whole cracker with caviar into his mouth, he almost immediately spit it out, right onto the ground.

But Penni was ready with a couple of napkins. She always came to the rescue. Still, he could feel that her mind was more on the new baby than on him. He was surprised to find he felt jealous. He wouldn't have thought he cared, and he would never admit that he cared, but the fact was he did care at that moment. He'd gotten used to being her first priority.

Finally the airline announced boarding. This flight was to be the longest of the trip—nine and a half hours. The flight attendants were tall, beautiful German girls.

Penni's face had grown radiant. Jaden had never seen her so pretty. He wondered if she'd been that way before he'd been brought home. They hadn't gone to Romania themselves—they'd hired a Romanian man to bring him to America. The first time Jaden had heard Penni crying in bed was when he'd cut up several sweaters she'd bought for him. After that she'd cried a lot. She about had a nervous breakdown when he burned his teddy bear's face. It had been the first thing they'd given him when they met him at the airport. He'd taken some charcoal lighter fluid and poured it on the teddy bear's face, and then put the bear into a pot in the sink. Apparently, he put on too much lighter fluid, because when he dropped a match on the teddy bear, it half exploded—*whoosh!*

The whole event left soot marks on the kitchen ceiling. Penni and Steve had been in bed already, and Jaden had gotten up only because he'd suddenly wanted to burn something.

He took the scorched teddy bear to bed with him. It was weird, and kind of embarrassing, but he liked stuffed animals. Penni and Steve didn't know that, though, so after he was ten, they never got him any again. He kept his stuffed animals in the back of his closet.

When Penni had seen the soot marks, she'd scolded him but also told him to never forget that she would always love him more than she loved anybody else in the world. Jaden knew that that was out the window now.

As the plane sped down the runway, Jaden crossed his arms and fingers and put on his sunglasses so nobody could tell how scared he was. The liftoff was smooth, and even as the plane reached flying altitude, there was no turbulence. Jaden uncrossed himself.

Steve leaned over Penni to ask him, "When are you going to take those sunglasses off?"

"When our last plane lands in Kyzylorda."

"What is it, some sort of lucky charm?"

"Yes," Jaden admitted.

He noticed three free seats in the middle section. He moved to there and lay down, feeling really happy that there was no turbulence. He played with his handheld Nintendo while lying on his back. He knew turbulence could happen at any time, but for the moment everything was fine. Then there was a touch of turbulence, but it went away. Maybe the sunglasses really were lucky. That is, he knew it didn't make sense to think so, but he couldn't bring himself to take them off. He did not want to die in an airplane.

Chapter Eight

The story was, Penni had seen his face on a waiting children list on the Internet, and she'd known immediately that she had to adopt him. She'd been married to someone else at the time. Jaden had been one year old in the picture but five in real life. Someone from his group home had lied and told the adoption agency that Jaden was still a baby. Then there was the divorce, and then Penni married Steve. So it had ended up taking three years to complete the adoption. That's why he'd been eight when he came to the United States and why Penni and Steve had thought he would be four. Jaden could tell that the Kazakh baby would belong to both Penni and Steve, while he mostly belonged to Penni. At least, that was the way he saw it. It was weird because before he came here, he'd been thrilled to be moving to America. He'd had all sorts of fantasies about how much he would love his new country. But somehow that wasn't the case. And that made him mad.

Anyway, inside every living organism were these holes called "ion channels," which allowed only certain atoms and molecules to pass through. Scientists had found electrical current associated with these channels. It was Jaden's belief that these mysterious ion channels controlled every part of life. Made your heart beat, made your kidneys clean your blood, made you breathe. Everything.

He would like to go to France someday to see *La Fée Électricité*, a painting about the history of electricity. It was huge, 624 square meters. If he were a painter, he would like to extend the painting to include the present. Currently it went up to 1937, and a lot had happened since then. He would add pictures of ion channels. His biggest and most important life goal was to learn the difference between life and death. Like, in a thing called "pulseless electrical activity," the body showed electrical activity even after the heart stopped beating. So were you alive or dead?

He stared up at the flimsy-looking plastic that contained the oxygen masks that would supposedly fall down if the cabin lost oxygen. He wondered how often maintenance workers checked to make sure those masks worked.

He felt somebody jiggle his feet and sat up to see Steve frowning at him. "What is it?" Jaden asked. He didn't like it when someone distracted him when he was thinking about something important, like oxygen.

"This adoption is something we're doing together, so let's do it together."

Huh? Jaden didn't get it. It's something they were

doing together, so they should do it together? Steve stared at him, then gestured his head like, *Come on.* Oh. They didn't like him being alone. Jaden climbed over the seats and went back to his window.

"Oh, honey, it didn't feel right without you here," Penni told him.

"Yeah, I know what you mean," Jaden said, though he knew no such thing.

"Ooh, I'm so worried about, well, it might be bad luck to say it. But you know."

Yeah, Jaden knew. Even he felt a little worried because of their adoption agency going out of business. And they were adopting from Kyzylorda, where Penni had told him few Americans had adopted. So basically, it was only hope that made them believe that their agency's in-country personnel would pick them up in Kyzylorda.

Their first stop in Kazakhstan was Almaty, the biggest city in the country. Jaden took off his sunglasses as they went through customs and headed for the waiting room. After the long flight, he wanted to move his legs, but there was nowhere much to go. The waiting area for all flights was a big room with a shiny white floor and row after row of connected seats. Most of the seats were filled. Jaden immediately noticed a group of women with babies.

"Mom, look, they must have just adopted."

"Let's go have a chat!" Penni said excitedly.

Jaden followed along. As soon as they reached the women, Steve stuck out his hand to shake with one of them. "I'm Steve Kincaid. Are you by some chance American? We're here to adopt and couldn't help noticing that you all have babies."

One of the ladies shook his hand and said, "Yes, we're all American. I'm Clara. What agency are you with?"

"One World Adoptions."

"Oh, I almost signed with them. I'm with Open Heart International." She gently jostled the baby in her arms, beaming down at him. "And this is Michael."

"I haven't heard of Open Heart," Penni said.

"They're a small agency but very good." Clara motioned to her baby. "The whole process took only a year."

"Really?" Penni exclaimed. "I'm jealous. We've been at it for longer."

"But for the moment we've put all negativity out of our thinking process," Steve added quickly.

"That's what you have to do when you're adopting," Clara agreed. "This is Nika, and her adoption took four years. She's suing her agency when she gets home."

"Four years!" Steve and Penni said simultaneously, shifting their attention to the woman beside Clara.

Jaden tuned out the talking and studied the babies. Three were Asian and two were not. He'd read up on it: Most babies adopted from Kazakhstan were Central Asian, Russian, or a mix. There were other ethnicities, but those were the main categories. Only one of the babies was asleep, one was awake and a little fussy, one was awake and staring blankly into space from his stroller, and two were crying despite their new mothers' attempts to calm them. He knelt in front of the one staring blankly.

"Hi," he said, as if he were talking to another twelve-year-old. The baby didn't even seem to notice him. "Baby, hi, adopted baby." Then the baby gazed at him, but blankly. "Are you a sleepy baby? It's very late."

One of the women knelt beside him. "Hi, I'm his mother. He isn't that demonstrative yet. He never laughs or cries."

"Can I touch him?"

"Sure."

Jaden poked gently at the baby's little face; it felt soft and doughy. He had never talked to or touched a baby before. Marty and Catherine had tried to get him to carry their baby, but he'd refused. Babies didn't seem quite human; plus, what if he broke a baby somehow? He glanced at the crying babies. The sound was already starting to annoy him. He hoped they didn't end up with a crier.

The blank-faced baby's mother tried tickling him under the chin, but he didn't respond. "I hope he's okay," the mother said. "His medical report said he was healthy. But I'm not sure he's bonded with me at all." She wrinkled her forehead and worriedly studied her new son, patting him softly on the chest.

"He does look healthy," Jaden said. He squeezed the baby's leg. "Ah, he feels strong. Maybe a wrestler someday."

"Can I ask you something that's none of my business?" the mother asked.

"What?"

"Are you adopted? I mean, I know it's none of my business."

"Yes, I am. I am. I'm Romanian. Romanian-American, I guess." He was surprised: He always thought he was incognito, since he was white and so were Penni and Steve.

"Oh, that's wonderful! Adoption is the most beautiful thing."

Jaden held her eyes briefly, then shifted his attention to the baby.

The baby was staring at Jaden as if Jaden were a statue or even a painting on a wall. It was like there was a slight glimmer of awareness, but nothing more.

Jaden stood up. The ladies with the crying babies already seemed stressed, and they hadn't even started their journey home yet. He felt bad for them, but he also felt bad for the poor babies. The babies probably didn't know what was going on, although who can say what someone that young knows? He hated how pompous doctors sounded when they assumed they knew what was going on in somebody else's head. They didn't know, and Jaden wished he could tell every adopted kid who had to talk to a doctor that the doctor didn't know. Only *you* know, and you don't have to tell them.

Jaden gazed around the big room. He couldn't see

any other kids. He thought he could feel the air of fatigue around just about everybody. It was like the whole room was filled with it, as if it were smoke or something. The chairs didn't appear very comfortable, but he sat in one anyway and tried to nap while Penni and Steve continued trading information with the women. Steve seemed merely curious, but Penni acted ravenous for information, her body leaning slightly forward and her face hyperalert. Jaden couldn't fall all the way asleep, but he did feel pleasantly half-asleep, the crying fading into the background. After a while he heard everyone saying good-bye, and he stood up groggily.

"Nice to meet you all," Penni was saying. "Good luck."

"Good luck," a couple of the women said back.

Jaden gave a small wave and watched the women push their strollers toward their gate to their new lives. He hoped the babies would grow up happy. He wondered what would become of the blank-faced baby and felt a sudden surge of protectiveness toward him, then a sudden surge of rage toward Penni and Steve for adopting him, even though they had nothing to do with those babies. But why hadn't they just given money to his mother so that she could raise him herself? He cried out, "Hey," and ran after the Americans.

They all stopped. He approached the woman with the blank-faced baby and said, "Let me give you my e-mail address. I want to know how your baby does."

"Oh," she said. She took out a pen, and he wrote down *RomJaden@att.net*.

"Thank you," he told her.

"No problem." But as Jaden watched her leave, he knew she would never e-mail him.

Penni and Steve decided to walk around the room for some exercise, but Jaden leaned back in a chair and gnawed vigorously on a straw he'd brought to chew on.

The woman next to him silently eyed the straw he was chewing, then said something sharply in another language.

The man on the other side of him said, "Excuse me." His accent was so thick, it took Jaden a moment to realize he was speaking English. "You are American? I might practice my English?"

"Yes," Jaden said, taking the straw out of his mouth.

"New York?"

"No, Illinois," Jaden answered. "Near Chicago."

The man nodded uncertainly. "You have seen Astana, our capital?"

"No."

"You should go. Astana is a symbol of the national idea statement."

This time it was for Jaden to nod uncertainly. The man was Central Asian, with dark, earnest eyes. He paused and his eyes went out of focus for a moment, as if he were thinking. "Los Angeles?" the man said. "Near where you live?"

"No, Chicago is the closest big city."

"I have not heard of this. Ahhhh, Americans have a sporty character, do they not?"

"Well." Jaden thought about that. "They do like sports."

"Good, good, all be well, isn't it?"

"Yes, well."

The woman next to him stood up, and the man smiled politely and opened out his palms. "My flight. I wish you pleasantries on your trip."

"You too. Nice to meet you."

"You're welcome. Good-bye."

"Bye."

The man got up and strode crisply off. Jaden chuckled to himself, then felt immediately surprised. He didn't laugh much, so it was always like he had to stop and take notice whenever he did.

When Penni and Steve sat back down, an hour had passed, with Jaden doing nothing but shaking his leg up and down and watching his feet as he shuffled them inside and out. Penni brushed hair out of his eyes. "Honey, why don't you get some sleep?" She put her arm around him and pulled him in. With her as a pillow, Jaden closed his eyes, but his mind was alert.

The sounds of announcements and the discomfort of the chair and the discomfort of Penni's shoulder kept him from falling asleep. And he couldn't stop thinking about the blank-faced baby. He hoped that child would be okay. He opened his eyes and stared at the reflections of tired people in the white floor. He imagined them all as babies, the whole room filled with babies.

Chapter Nine

When their flight was finally announced, Jaden was still alert. Penni had fallen asleep leaning against Jaden's shoulder. They trudged to the plane, a small one. Penni sat with him on one side of the plane, and Steve sat across the aisle. The plane had propellers, which made Jaden nervous. He slipped his sunglasses back on. He didn't see anyone on the flight who looked like they might be American. He was reminded again that only a small number of Americans had ever adopted from Kyzylorda, according to Penni.

She'd been keeping in touch with the last woman who'd traveled there to adopt. That woman had come home without a baby, saying the orphanage had shown her only "brain-dead" children. Penni and Steve absolutely did not want a special-needs child. Jaden knew that was because he was all they could handle. But, in general, the staff at Kyzylorda baby house were known to take good care of its babies, and the process was usually smooth.

Penni and Jaden played gin rummy while Steve snored. Steve kept snoring all during the landing. Penni had to shake him awake after the plane taxied to the gate. When they got off the plane, her face was lit up with excitement. It was the same face she'd greeted Jaden with at the Chicago airport when he first came to America.

Because Penni and Steve hadn't actually traveled to Romania, his adoption was somehow less legitimate to Jaden. He couldn't remember the Romanian guy's name who'd brought him over on the plane. All he remembered was that a number of times during the flight the man had yelled at him.

"We're here!" Steve suddenly announced, as if he were telling them something they didn't know.

Jaden took off his sunglasses at last and could feel his pulse speed up as they made their way through the airport. He'd studied a bit of Russian with a CD in preparation for their trip. The conversations overheard on the plane sounded like both Russian and what he assumed was Kazakh. Kyzylorda was about 70 percent Kazakh; the Kazakhs were Central Asian. Jaden had never been in the racial minority before. He was surprised how different it made him feel, like maybe people wouldn't be nice to him. He also worried that people wouldn't be nice to him when they found out he was adopted, so he was glad he looked like he could possibly be the biological son of Steve and Penni. His hazel eyes were the same color as Penni's, and they both had wavy brown hair. He wondered how that lady in the airport had known he was adopted.

The Kyzylorda airport was small—like, maybe

four or five times the size of their house—and it had only one runway. They got their baggage in the luggage dump room and stepped outside. "There's no one here," Steve finally said, though it was obvious.

The wind was blowing hard. A few weeks ago Steve had gotten in touch with a Peace Corps worker who was stationed in Kyzylorda, and that guy had said the wind blew constantly here. The day was hot and bright. Dust pinged on Jaden's face.

"Now what should we do?" Penni asked Steve worriedly. Jaden couldn't see a single person.

Then suddenly a car was parking, and a woman got out and started running toward them. She cried out, "Kincaid! Kincaid!"

She was holding a sign with their last name on it, except spelled "Kencaid." An old man limped after her. "I am sorry we were late," she said. "Hello, nice to meet you. I am Akerke, and that is your driver, Sam. He is Turkish but speaks many languages." She gestured toward the man, who had not yet caught up to her. "I am very good with the English, and Sam also speaks." Sam finally caught up with her, and she smiled brightly at him. "Sam learned English in Michigan, did I say that right?" Actually, she pronounced it "Meesheegon."

"I have been to America," Sam said grumpily. "I have nephew there. He got married. I went to wedding. In America, if you have guest, you watch TV together. In Kazakhstan, if you have guest, you talk to him. Huh!"

"He is very good driver," Akerke said happily. "First let me give you this." She took out an old bulky cell phone and handed it to Steve. "This you must carry at all times so I may reach you and you may reach me. My number is listed in phone already. Come. We will take your luggage." Then she added, "Please hurry," as if they were the ones who were late.

Sam stared at the three giant suitcases. He grasped two of them and began rolling them away while muttering, "Even the child has a big luggage. What does a child need with a big luggage?"

"A child has many items he will need," Akerke said, as if rebuking him. She put her arm around Jaden. "I understand fully well. You are Daniel, are you not?"

"Jaden."

"Yes," said Akerke. "As I meant. I was thinking of the man in the Peace Corps. His name is Daniel. He said he knows you?"

"We've communicated with him," Steve said. "Indeed, we've communicated more with him than with our adoption agency."

Akerke smiled maternally at Jaden. "And when will you get married?"

"Well," Jaden said. "Well, I don't know. I'm twelve years old."

"Is good age," Akerke said approvingly, adding, "I will sit in back to talk to your parents."

The car was an old, bright-red Mercedes. Jaden felt like a grown-up sitting in front. Then Sam squealed out of the parking lot. Even though at home in Illinois Jaden would sit only in the middle in back, now he didn't care where he sat. None of the rules from back home mattered here in Kazakhstan.

"I will come get you at your apartment this evening, and you will choose your baby. The baby house director will stay late just for you."

Jaden whipped around, saw Penni and Steve looking at each other in alarm. "But . . . we were already sent a referral for a baby. A specific baby," Steve said.

Akerke opened her mouth and even moved her lips, but no words came out.

"We were sent a referral," Steve said again. "The boy's name is Bahytzhan. Here, I have a picture." He took out his wallet and showed Akerke the photo.

"Bahytzhan," Akerke said. "I have met him. He has been adopted by German family. But we will find for you even more beautiful baby."

The trip was already a disaster. Jaden had to admit that even he had kind of gotten used to the picture of the baby. In Bahytzhan's picture, his little forehead was wrinkled with worry. Jaden knew just how he felt: Bahytzhan didn't have a mother, and he was worried about it.

Penni's and Steve's mouths were both hanging open. "Bahytzhan is gone?" Penni asked. "But he was offered to us. We accepted his referral. We were expecting him to be our son." Then she said with the assertiveness she occasionally pulled out of a hat, "I'm *still* expecting it."

"We will get you very nice baby," Akerke replied. "Better than Bahytzhan."

"You don't understand what we're saying. We came all the way here just for Bahytzhan," Steve said.

"We were told it was all set," Penni added, again assertively. "He's the baby I came for, and he's the baby I want."

Apropos of nothing, Sam said to Jaden, "Everything in America is practical. For instance, there are no potholes."

"Actually, a lot of potholes are formed in the United States every year from the weather," Jaden said. "We get them where we live too."

"What does a young boy know of potholes?"

"We visit government offices once in a while for field trips at school, so I know about potholes that way," Jaden said, studying Sam's profile. He had wrinkled, dark skin. A lot of his wrinkles were smile lines, which seemed like a good thing.

"Your school teaches you about potholes instead of arithmetic?"

"No, we learn that, too."

"Potholes and arithmetic. What is the world coming to?" Sam shook his head, as if determined to be unhappy.

"Jaden," said Akerke, "Sam has many opinions. But later you will like it to talk to him. He reminds me of my uncle."

"Hold on a second," Steve said. Jaden could hear his voice getting tense. He was used to that voice. "How did Bahytzhan get adopted? We came here to adopt him. That's what we came for, and only that. We didn't come to choose a baby."

"You must accept another beautiful baby," Akerke said patiently. "Bahytzhan was beautiful baby, yes, but he was not *most* beautiful. There are others. You will see. Bahytzhan cried many times. Once he spent two hours crying during bonding period. Beautiful, yes, but he was difficult baby."

Penni was sitting with her mouth hanging open again, stunned. She always had so much faith that everything would work out if you were just a good person, and now she looked completely defeated. "It's impossible," Penni said at last. "Difficult or not, we came for him. How can someone else have adopted him? Why did you let that happen?"

"Is baby house director who decides this." Akerke took a big breath. "I do not know everything how this happened. But I tell you that Bahytzhan is gone. He is gone." Her expression grew worried. "Just the same, we will need to go forward."

Jaden waited to see how Penni and Steve would react.

Out of nowhere Sam mused, "Americans have a lot of money, but I once had much more. I had so much money, it reached the ceiling in my home."

He jerked his head sharply at Jaden. "Do you believe me?"

"Sure," Jaden said.

"It is true!" Sam cried out, as if Jaden had said he didn't believe it.

Outside the car, the landscape was barren—brown dirt, faded plants, and gray-green bushes and trees. Occasionally Jaden saw a shepherd and sheep. One time they passed a shepherd with several double-hump camels ambling close to the road. Jaden had never seen a camel outside a zoo. He opened his window. The warm air blew into his face, but he also felt those little pings from the dust. He raised the window and let his mind wander.

Chapter Ten

The vast steppes were mesmerizing; Jaden lost track of time. He'd read the definition of "steppe" in the dictionary before they left. It meant "a large area of flat, unforested grassland in southeastern Europe or Siberia."

Closer to the city, some half-built buildings blended into the landscape. Soon, Sam turned down an unpaved road. A camel rummaged through a garbage bin, and a pack of dogs scampered across an empty lot. There was row after row of similar buildings. Penni had told Jaden they would be staying in

housing left over from when Kazakhstan was part of the Soviet Union.

Some of the roads Sam drove down were paved; huge sinkholes marred the asphalt. All over the roads were patches of white, but it wasn't cold enough for snow. "Where does the white stuff come from?" Jaden asked.

"Is salt from the Aral Sea," Akerke said eagerly, as if happy not to be talking about the adoption.

There was also broken glass everywhere. Some homes had missing walls, some had makeshift tin roofs. Even though everything Jaden could see was ugly, he felt that it was exciting somehow, a little bit magical, like anything could happen here, unlike in America, where every day was the same.

Then they passed a couple of Kazakh people with piles of watermelons on blankets. He wondered how much the watermelons cost. A good watermelon could pretty much make your day.

At last they came to a row of tan five-story apartment buildings that stretched as far as Jaden could

see. All the same. Many of the curtains were blue. Antennas and satellite dishes sprouted from the tops of the buildings.

There were no doors that Jaden could see. The main vegetation was weeds.

Sam turned down an alley and pulled to a stop in front of a blue door with a big crack making its way up the center. "This will be your apartment," Akerke said.

They all got out, and Sam opened the trunk, again taking two of the suitcases and leaving the last for Akerke.

"Let me take that," Steve said.

Akerke waved him off. "Is my job."

"Why do Americans have such big luggages?" Sam asked. "They must own many things. Give me a toothbrush and three shirts and I am ready to go anywhere." He shot a glance at Jaden—he seemed to have glommed on to Jaden. "Huh?"

"We have gifts and baby things, and I brought some granola," Jaden explained.

"What is this?"

"Excuse me?" asked Jaden.

"What is this? You just said it."

"Granola?"

"Yes."

"It's nuts and grains and honey. You eat it with milk."

Sam nodded knowingly. "Ah, cereal. Leave it to an American to bring cereal to Kazakhstan."

"What do you mean?" Jaden asked.

"Americans like to bring America with them wherever they go. Why not eat Kazakh cereal, eh? Tell me that."

"Granola is kind of special cereal."

Sam looked interested. "Eh?"

Several numbered push buttons were on the foyer door. Akerke punched in the code and said, "One, six, three, two. Do not forget or all will be lost."

Penni said, "One, six, three, two. One, six, three, two. One, six, three, two. Got it."

Sam grunted and lifted the two suitcases up the crumbling steps. At one point one of the wheels got stuck in a hole.

"I can help, Sam," Steve said.

"Do not insult me."

"Seriously," Steve answered, "let me take them."

"You must not insult me, though you pay my salary," Sam replied.

When they reached the fifth floor, Sam rested his hands on his knees and breathed deeply several times. "Ah," he said. "Ahhhh. Cereal. Thrilling cereal."

"Special cereal," Jaden corrected him.

Akerke jiggled a key in the lock for a minute. Then she opened the door. Right away there was another door, less than a foot from the first one. Sam stayed at the threshold while the rest of them wandered from room to room. The apartment had two bedrooms, with a queen-size bed in one and a twin bed in the other; a large living room; a bathroom; and a large kitchen with a table and chairs.

Out the window in the room with the twin bed,

Jaden was happy to see that you could view the steppe way beyond the alley.

"Is fine?" Akerke asked.

"It's perfect," Penni said.

"Is very nice," Akerke said happily. She was just about the happiest person Jaden had ever met. "Is very modern," she continued. "In my country many people still eat and sleep on floor, but here you may eat and sleep as you do in America." She smiled widely, truly happy. "You have cable and may watch all the television. Many stations." She gave a quick, smiling nod of her head after she said that. "And there are dishes for eating." Another happy nod of her head. "Is very much okay, I think."

"Oh, yes, of course," Penni said. "Absolutely."

"Quite acceptable," Steve said. "We were expecting worse."

"And why is this?" Akerke asked. She seemed a little insulted.

"We'd read up on the poverty here," Steve said.

"It's fine," Penni added quickly. "Absolutely."

"Absolutely," Akerke repeated. "I have always liked that word. The Americans have many fine words. Now, can you be waiting downstairs at seven?"

"Yes, of course," Steve said.

Akerke and Sam left, and Steve took Penni in his arms. "Don't worry, we'll ask again about Bahytzhan. Maybe there's some kind of mistake," he said.

"In my heart he's already ours." She was pressing her cheek into Steve's shoulder.

"I know. I know. We'll get everything straightened out when we go to the baby house."

Jaden decided to take a nap while Penni and Steve went grocery shopping. First of all, he hadn't gotten his twelve hours of sleep, and second of all, he'd been with Penni and Steve for thirty-five straight hours, and that was more than enough. "If we don't find a store, I guess we're having watermelon for dinner," Steve said.

"I saw a market on the way here," Penni said. "I think we can find it."

After Penni and Steve left, Jaden took off his shoes

and collapsed onto his bed. He stared at the ceiling for about ten seconds, then decided to catch up with Penni and Steve. He wanted to see what kind of food they had here, so he could choose his own groceries. He tied his sneakers back up, grabbed a Russian-English dictionary, and dashed out the front door. He'd thought about bringing a Kazakh dictionary, but though most Kazakhs spoke their language, some did not. Plus, 30 percent of the people in Kyzylorda weren't Kazakh. And Penni had told him that virtually everyone here spoke Russian.

He made his way slowly down the crumbly steps. When he was almost at the bottom, a step crumbled under his foot, and he almost fell. Boy, in America that would be a lawsuit waiting to happen.

Once outside, he glanced both ways. Penni and Steve weren't anywhere. Where had they gone so quickly? Their building was in the middle of the block, so he had to choose right or left. He chose right and started jogging down the alley, in the same direction they'd driven here from.

Chapter Eleven

When Jaden got to the street, he again looked both ways and still didn't see Penni and Steve. He considered running back to the other end of the alley, though he knew it would be too late to find them by now. So he hurried toward the front of the buildings. But when he got there, no luck. And dang it, he didn't have a key to the apartment.

Jaden hadn't seen anything resembling a market on the way here. But there were watermelon vendors. He opened up the dictionary and approached one of them. The woman said something that he of course didn't understand.

"*Produktoviyj magazin?*" Jaden asked.

The woman now began talking quickly.

"*Produktoviyj magazin?*" Jaden said again, tilting his head a little so the woman knew he was asking a question. Then he pointed in a random direction and said, "*Produktoviyj magazin?*" again. He pointed at himself. "*Amerikanets.*"

The woman called out to another vendor. "American!" She and the other vendor talked for a bit and seemed to have forgotten about him, but then the woman pointed in a direction and said slowly, "*Produktoviyj magazin.*"

"*Spasiba,*" Jaden said. "*Da svidaniya.*" He set off in the direction the woman had indicated, memorizing landmarks. He walked through row after row of old Soviet apartment buildings that looked a lot like the one they were staying in. After about fifteen minutes he paused and stood on a corner. There was a shaggy two-hump camel right in his path. The camel started to come directly toward Jaden as if intrigued by him. He wouldn't have thought he'd be scared of a camel, but he was.

Jaden trotted across the street, but the camel came galloping toward him. Jaden broke into a run. When he was out of breath, he looked back, and the camel was standing about ten feet away, watching him. He took a few backward steps, and the camel didn't follow, so he moved away toward another vendor.

This vendor was selling huge squash as well as watermelons. Yuck, he hated squash. He asked again for a grocery store. The vendor pointed in a different direction from the one he was going in. So should he trust her? He paused, then decided he would go in the direction she pointed but keep careful track of where he was. He took note of an empty lot with a pile of colorful boxes sitting on it. That would be his landmark. He set off again, and after exactly eleven minutes he came to a grocery store. It was very small, and there was a woman churning butter at the entrance. He had read that there were currency exchanges all over, including in many stores, but there was probably none here—it was too small. He went in anyway. The store was basically a wooden shack with two aisles.

He didn't see any shopping baskets. He picked up a small bag of almonds and a cheese, tomato, and cucumber salad in a plastic bag. In general he didn't like vegetables, but he loved cheese a lot. When he first got to America, it was almost all he ate some days. He grabbed an uncut loaf of bread and a big block of white cheese and set the items on the counter in front of the cashier. She said something in what he thought was Russian.

Jaden took out a crisp hundred-dollar bill Penni had given him for a situation exactly like this and showed it to her. *"Ya Amerikanets,"* he said.

The cashier took the bill and held it up to the light from the window. She stepped outside and had an emotional exchange of words with the butter churner, and then she put the bill into a metal box and handed Jaden some tenge—Kazakh money.

Jaden stepped out of the store feeling quite successful. He checked his watch and walked for eleven minutes, but he didn't see the dirt lot with colored boxes. Huh. He was positive he hadn't passed it yet. So he set off again, but after five more minutes he stopped and faced the opposite direction. He went all the way back to the store, and then walked back in the direction of the dirt lot. But after twenty minutes he hadn't passed it. This wasn't possible.

Jaden turned around in a circle. It wasn't that nothing looked familiar. The trouble was, *everything* looked familiar. All the buildings were so similar. He pulled out his phone. No charge. He felt panic rising up in him, but it was quickly replaced by something else: He was hungry, and that took precedence, as always. He sat down in a lot and ripped off a piece of bread, then ripped off a chunk of cheese and ate the two together. It was so good, he closed his eyes so he could concentrate on the taste.

Someone yelled, so he opened his eyes and saw a woman in spiky heels standing about ten feet away, hanging back as if he were dangerous. Jaden braced himself—for what, he didn't know. He said, *"Amerikanets,"* and pointed at his chest. That stopped her for a second, but then she yelled "No gypsies!" in English. Sometimes in Romania he'd been called a gypsy by strangers, but he didn't know if he really had gypsy blood or not.

Jaden assessed his situation. The cheese and bread were so good, he felt optimistic. He returned to the store yet again, then walked for eleven minutes at the same speed at which he thought he'd been traveling in the first place. At eleven minutes he stopped and went left.

He kept going until a row of buildings stopped him. He didn't have the slightest idea where to go now. He wondered: Would he now be able to escape from Penni and Steve, and was that actually what he wanted? Then he pulled out his dictionary again and found "I'm lost" in the phrase section. *Ya zabludilsya.*

He spotted a watermelon vendor who he might or might not have seen earlier. He approached her and said, *"Ya zabludilsya. Amerikanets."*

The woman said something to him, but he didn't understand this either.

Jaden checked his dictionary again. *"Politsiya?"* Maybe the police could help him.

The woman pointed in a direction and said, *"Politsiya."*

Jaden hated to go anywhere at all. He might end up even farther from home base. But he had no choice. *"Spasiba,"* he told the woman before he set off again. He walked and walked but didn't see anything that seemed like a police station. He did come to a huge market, though, row after row of "stores." Each store was basically four poles with a tarp or old wood on top. It reminded him of a flea market he'd been to once when he, Penni, and Steve were visiting relatives in California.

Jaden saw shoes, clothes, and linens. Also, there were women with scarfs on their head who were bent over beat-up sewing machines, mending pants or waiting for something to do. Near a music stand, a man as old as Sam was dancing to some Kazakh music that sounded like it'd been infused with a hip-hop beat. The old man was pretty spry and kept the beat with his feet very well.

Then Jaden saw what he thought was a security guard also watching the dancing. The man was dressed in camouflage and had a rifle slung over his shoulder. Jaden hurried to him.

"Amerikanets!" he cried out, pointing to himself. *"Ya zabludilsya!"*

The man peered around, as if searching for Jaden's parents or for someone to help. He spoke in Russian to Jaden, but once again Jaden didn't understand. He held out his dictionary, as if that would explain everything to the security guard.

"I would like help," Jaden said. *"Ya zabludilsya."*

The guard nodded to Jaden to follow him as he moved quickly through the maze of vendors. Eventually he spotted who he wanted, a woman selling bed linens. He spoke to her for a moment, and then she said to Jaden, "You are lost."

Relief flooded through Jaden—he must have wanted to be found worse than he thought. *"Da,"* he said. "Yes."

"Where are your parents?"

"I don't know."

"Shopping here?"

"No, I don't know where they are. I'm completely lost."

The woman paused thoughtfully. She and the man spoke again, and then the man left. "Where do you stay?"

"In a building, but I don't know where it is. We just arrived today. We're adopting a baby from the baby house."

"Ah, baby house." The woman's face became hopeful. "Do you have money?"

Jaden reached into his pocket and pulled out the tenge. The woman's face lit up, and she gently pulled several bills from Jaden's hand and left some others.

"My son will take you to baby house." She called out "Arystan," and a young man with slicked-back hair sauntered up. She spoke to him sharply, and he nodded. "Go with him. He will take you."

Jaden followed him to a street, and they came to a beat-up blue car. Arystan got behind the wheel, and Jaden got into the passenger side after a struggle with the dented door.

Arystan backed up wildly, braked, and screeched forward. Jaden rummaged around for a seat belt, but there was none. His side of the car scraped against a parked automobile, but Arystan didn't react at all.

Neither of them talked. Eventually the car pulled up to a mural of two parents holding hands with a young child. Arystan grunted and indicated with his head that they'd arrived. Jaden said, *"Spasiba, da svidanya."*

Arystan shrugged, and the second Jaden was out, the car screeched away.

Past a gate, Jaden saw several buildings. A bunch of toddlers were standing around a courtyard with what he assumed were a couple of baby house caretakers. He stared at the children. When he was the age of some of them, he still had a mother.

"Amerikanets," he said to one of the caretakers, pointing at himself. *"Ya zabludilsya.* My parents are adopting."

The woman said something to him, but of course Jaden had no idea what. She pointed to a door. Jaden went inside; all was quiet. The smell of bleach filled the air. There was also a yeasty smell, like someone had baked bread at some point in the last few hours. He peeked inside a room with an open door and saw another woman sitting behind a desk. The woman said something sharply to him.

"Amerikanets," he said, pointing at himself. *"Ya zabludilsya."*

"Zabludilsya?"

"Da," Jaden answered.

"Did—you—go *Amerikanskoye posol'stvo?"*

Jaden didn't know what to say. "My parents are adopting from here. Adoption. Parents."

"Oh! Adoption! Parents, parents, parents." She picked up a phone, punched in some numbers, and spoke in Kazakh into the phone. Then she gestured for Jaden to take the receiver.

Jaden took it eagerly. "Hello?" he said.

"Good day. This is Akerke."

"Akerke! It's Jaden. I got lost, and someone drove me to the baby house. My parents are probably worried."

"Yes, I have heard from them. You may wait. I will be at the baby house soon. You must not bother the director of baby house again. She is not pleased. Maybe can you sit outside. Yes, outside is good idea. Good-bye."

"Good-bye."

"*Spasiba*," Jaden said to the director.

The woman made a motion with a hand and said, "Shoo. Shoo."

Chapter Twelve

Jaden went outside and sat on the steps, where he could see the toddlers playing. The pavement was cracked and the playground was old and rusty. There were electrical wires hanging down. A pool had been installed, but it was empty and Jaden saw there was no drain. Cats roamed the grounds.

Jaden had never really paid much attention to young kids before. Some of the ones here were cute. But some of them seemed untamed, like animals in a forest, running into one another and grunting instead of talking.

One little boy with a severe case of bedhead trotted up to Jaden and made some grunting noises. They weren't grunts exactly. Jaden wasn't sure what they were. He'd never heard such noises coming from a person. They were kind of moans mixed with grunts and growls and occasional mumbles. The boy waved his arms in the air, as if trying to make Jaden understand something. He was an extremely beautiful boy, with huge slanting eyes and long, thick black hair, while the other boys had shorter hair. The kid's skin almost glowed. But though he seemed healthy, there was also something fragile about him. For one thing, he was very thin, maybe as thin as Jaden had once been.

All of a sudden, a woman came out and clapped her hands three times, hard, and all the toddlers went running inside. Jaden was alone. Two women dragged a mattress from one of the buildings, threw it into the swimming pool, poured gas on it, and set it on fire. Jaden had no idea what they were doing. He watched while the mattress burned. Finally he saw Penni, Steve, and Akerke. Penni ran up and threw her arms around him, and he hugged her back, which he usually tried to avoid.

"We were so worried," Penni said, placing her palm on his forehead as if he had a fever. "We were ready to report a missing child to the American Embassy."

"I decided to go with you to the market, but when I got downstairs, I couldn't find you."

"Don't wander off by yourself anymore, do you hear me?" Penni hugged him again.

"You guys disappeared so fast," Jaden said.

Akerke interrupted. "We must go inside. We would not want to be late to see director."

They followed her into the small room where Jaden had found the woman who'd called Akerke. Her seat was empty now. There were several folding chairs along the wall, and Akerke told them to sit down while she herself rushed off. "Right after we're introduced, we need to start this meeting by finding out what happened to Bahytzhan," Steve said. He pushed his glasses up his nose two times, like he did whenever he was super-serious about something.

Jaden looked around, as he hadn't noticed much his first time in there. The room was nothing special. There was a wall of windows with blinds, and in front of another wall was a wooden desk, a shelf, and a filing cabinet. A picture of some old guy in a suit in front of the Kazakh flag hung on a wall. A boombox sat on a shelf. There was another door leading to who knows where, and the folding chairs where Akerke told them to sit. There was also a couch. Jaden wondered who got to sit there.

Akerke returned with the woman. Jaden waited for Akerke to introduce everyone, but instead the woman said something sharply. Akerke scrunched up her forehead worriedly and said, "The director would like to know how you lost your son today."

"I wandered off on my own," Jaden said. "They thought I was staying in the apartment."

"She would like to hear from your parents," Akerke scolded Jaden.

"We were going to a market I had seen on the drive over from the airport," Penni said quickly. "Jaden said he wanted to rest after the long flight, so we left him to nap. We'd heard from our agency that when you need a ride, you can just wave your hand at any car, and they'll drive you for a price. So we did that in the alley. Then Jaden went out on his own, and apparently he got lost."

"She is worried you will lose the baby."

"Lose the baby?" Steve said. "Tell her that's ridiculous."

"I cannot say that to her," Akerke said sternly.

"Ridiculous? What is ridiculous?" the director asked. Jaden wished his phone was charged so he could take a picture of her.

Akerke said something to the director. They talked back and forth for a few minutes, and then the director nodded and left the room. Akerke smiled at last. "She accepts your answer."

The director shouted something from the hallway. Steve said to Akerke in his best authoritative voice, "About Bahytzhan. We have some questions we need to ask the director."

But he didn't get a chance to ask questions, because a scrawny woman came in carrying a scrawny baby. The woman held out the baby casually, almost like it was a stuffed toy rather than a real person. Though the weather was warm today, the baby had two or three outfits on. The scrawny woman yawned and spoke to Akerke, after which Akerke said to Penni and Steve, "Thirteen months old. Boy."

Jaden, Penni, and Steve stared at one another in surprise.

The woman spoke again, and then the director came back in. Akerke translated: "Motor skills below normal. Kidney . . . kidney is not so good . . . mother had syphilis . . . no sign of disease in child."

Then everybody turned to Penni and Steve.

"Wait, are we—we're deciding *now*?" Penni sputtered.

"Yes, of course," Akerke replied matter-of-factly.

"Now, let's slow down here," Steve said. "We wanted to converse first about our referral. Are you sure Bahytzhan has been adopted? We were specifically told we had a referral for a specific baby. We gave his information and picture to a doctor in America to approve. That's who we came for . . . whom."

"You must move on from Bahytzhan," Akerke said, her voice firm.

Jaden wondered how you could "move on" from something like this. How do you move on from a child you felt you already loved? He could see Penni and Steve were stressed. Even he was starting to feel stressed. The woman with the baby hurried out, and another woman with a different baby replaced her. The new woman had a scarf covering her hair and smiled at Jaden and held the baby close to herself. Penni's mouth fell open. Jaden glanced at Steve; his mouth was open too. Akerke spoke with this new woman.

"Is eighteen months old boy . . . does not crawl yet but will crawl soon . . . otherwise healthy." Akerke seemed to add of her own accord, "Is beautiful baby."

This baby had a lot of black hair and was chubby and cute. His face was blank, like he didn't see anything at all as he stared into the air. Still, as far as Jaden could tell, he was a good baby. But he didn't really know how to judge what a good baby was.

And choosing now? Things were moving too fast. It was all so unreasonable, it had started to feel surreal to Jaden. He didn't see how you could decide something important like this after seeing a baby for a minute, if that long. By now Penni was digging her nails into her upper arm like she did sometimes when she was extremely tense or upset.

But the woman was already leaving with the cute baby. The director spoke to Akerke, who spoke to Penni and Steve. "Another couple has passed that boy in hallway last week and would like to adopt him, but director has said you have first choice because other couple has already started bonding with different baby. How is my English?"

"We comprehend," Steve said.

The first woman came in with yet another baby. She held it in the air as if she didn't want it close to her. This baby was also bundled up, and he or she was wearing a beret.

"Fourteen months old girl . . . walking . . . talking . . . is healthy baby."

But Jaden thought the baby looked wrong. She wasn't symmetrical. Her right eye was noticeably higher than her left eye, and her right nostril was noticeably higher than the left. But was he being unfair? She was also blank faced.

When Penni and Steve met eyes but didn't speak, the woman rushed out. Akerke said, "Next will be last baby. Is one more baby to show you."

Jaden looked around the plain office again. Here was this completely generic office, and yet lives were being changed in here.

The final baby was brought in. The baby's head was falling to the side, as if it was too heavy for the neck to support. Its thin limbs fluttered in the air as if the baby had no control over them. Penni started to speak, but then the woman took the baby out of the office without talking to Akerke, as if bringing that baby in was just a formality. Jaden stared after them. He hoped someone would adopt that child.

Penni and Steve spoke quietly to each other for a moment. Jaden heard Penni say to Steve, "What can we do? Apparently, we have to decide *now*. I actually read about this type of situation on a Yahoo group— they said that you hardly have any time to decide."

Steve stuck out his lower jaw with determination. "Then we have to decide before this gets even worse." He asked loudly, "May we see the second one again?" Penni's eyes opened wide in surprise, but Jaden thought it was good for Steve to act with determination and abandon Bahytzhan. Bahytzhan was gone. Bahytzhan had probably come into this room, gotten accepted, and then his path had diverged from theirs.

Akerke spoke to the director. The director yelled

out, and a minute later the second baby was brought back in. Jaden thought he was very cute, his eyes huge and gray. The woman spoke in Russian but watched Penni and Steve as she talked. When she finished talking, she held the baby extra close and smiled.

Akerke translated. "I tell you again. Fifteen months old. Though he cannot walk yet, he can get up and hold table and stand. Does not speak yet. I think this is best baby. I would take this baby, and the director believes this is very good baby. The other couple will get this baby if you do not want him."

"I thought you said he was eighteen months," Steve said.

"Is fifteen."

"But you just told us—" Steve said.

Jaden's head was spinning. Akerke had definitely said eighteen months the first time. "How do you know the director likes him?" he piped up.

"The nurse has told me. The director knows the babies very well."

"I don't care about his age! May I hold him?" asked Penni politely, standing up.

"Is fine," said Akerke.

Penni took the baby, who didn't show any sign that he was now being held by someone new. "What's his name?"

Akerke said, "Is Ramazan."

"Ramazan," said Penni to the baby. "Fifteen months old. Ramazan, what a handsome boy. Is Ramazan a happy boy today?"

Ramazan stared at Penni's lips. Jaden squeezed the baby's leg; he didn't feel strong like the baby from the airport. But what did Jaden know about legs?

"You must accept him. Is no more babies," Akerke said.

Ramazan's blankness made Jaden feel that the baby was vulnerable, as if nobody had ever responded to his cries, and so he had learned not to cry. Jaden knew what that was like. Ramazan was probably used to being handed off from one person to another. *Poor little guy,* Jaden thought, but then he immediately went full circle and felt a stab of jealousy. He could tell they were going to end up with Ramazan. How was that fair when Jaden had languished in group homes for four years?

"Do I get a vote?" Jaden asked bitterly. Without waiting for an answer, he blurted out, "I don't like him, Mom."

"You don't?" Penni leaned toward Jaden. "That's important."

"Still, you must decide," Akerke said urgently. "Please do not anger director, or you can end up with nothing."

Jaden spoke up again. "Why don't we go to a different baby house?"

"Is no more baby house in Kyzylorda," Akerke said. "Jaden, I must talk to your parents." Akerke stood up to get closer to Penni.

Penni was frowning hard. "But if none of them is right—"

"You cannot tell who is right or wrong. Only in time you will see."

"But he seems so, well, vacant."

"What is that?"

"I mean he doesn't notice or respond to anything, on top of which we were ready for Bahytzhan. He'd looked very emotional from his picture. In our minds we've bonded with Bahytzhan," Penni explained. "I'm just floored."

"What is floored?"

"It's really, really surprised. We thought we were coming for Bahytzhan. And this baby, he's so unresponsive. Isn't that a sign of autism?"

Jaden's mind suddenly spun full circle again. He felt like he had no control over his feelings. "Mom, I know I just said I don't like him, but this is the best baby. I—"

Akerke interrupted. "What is there for him to be emotional about at this moment? Is beautiful baby, this one. Is no choice of Bahytzhan anymore."

"What if I would be the wrong mother for him?" Penni wailed.

Steve touched her arm. "Now, wait a minute, Pen.

I like him the best. I'm experiencing some partiality toward this one."

"When Jaden arrived, I was immediately filled with love," Penni said.

Jaden remembered her at the airport picking him up, how lit up her face was when she met him. He, on the other hand, immediately decided he didn't trust them. He thought they would send him to another house.

"Is not fair to compare him to your son. Each child is different," Akerke argued. "I say to you now that you will not see any more babies. I say to you that you must decide or go back to America with no baby. Is no more babies. Only toddlers."

Toddlers? Jaden thought of the growling boy. "I saw a toddler that I liked," he said.

"Really?" Penni asked, still holding Ramazan. "Where?"

"No," Steve said immediately. "We want a *baby*. Penni, we have conversed about this for hundreds of hours. Literally. And we agreed we want a *baby*."

"Mom," Jaden said. "Come see the toddler. Please?"

Penni looked worriedly from Jaden to Steve. "How can I decide so quickly?" She burst into tears. "And all these babies. Who will adopt them?"

"I feel for all the babies, all the children who're here," Steve said, his voice softer. "But that doesn't make them the right one for us." He stroked Penni's face. "But, honey, I think this Ramazan comes the closest. I think we would bond with any of them, actually, but this one is just what we were looking for." Then Steve went into Mr. Spock mode, like he did sometimes. "The paradoxical aspect of this experience is that the overpowering propensity is to be emotional, and yet we must also be detached and businesslike. Upon suspending one's emotions, one finds that Ramazan is indeed the correct baby."

"But . . . ," Penni said. Then she leaned over and touched the baby's nose with her own before lifting her head again. "He *is* lovely. His eyes . . ."

"His eyes are very beautiful," Akerke agreed eagerly.

Penni's face was screwed into a frown. "Well—I don't—I mean—I mean all right, this one then. He's my favorite." She kissed the baby's head. Then she asked Akerke, "What will happen to the others?"

"Some will be adopted. Some will not."

"It's very hard to think about that," Penni said.

"It's so random," Jaden blurted out. "You come into this rinky-dink office, and an hour later you have a whole different future." That's kind of what had happened to him.

"Yes!" Penni exclaimed. "It's mind-boggling." She rubbed her cheek on the baby's, then said to him, "Your path is about to be altered, and ours, too." Ramazan was staring at her lips again.

Akerke smiled happily. "Ramazan is one of best babies I have ever seen." She nodded her head up and down. She reminded Jaden of a bobblehead doll.

Akerke and the director spoke to each other, the

director's voice growing angry. Akerke replied in a soothing voice, talking and talking. Finally the director smiled slightly, apparently appeased.

"The director has said you must not kiss the baby or breathe so close to him in case you have germs," Akerke told Penni. "They had flu last month." But she smiled happily. "Tomorrow you have appointment to see your baby at one thirty." Akerke alone seemed ecstatic.

Chapter Thirteen

That night Jaden sat by his open bedroom window after Penni and Steve had fallen asleep. He thought about the day. For Akerke and the director, it was perhaps just another day. But for his family, it was one unlike any they'd ever had. The idea of accepting a baby after a single minute was plain nuts. He thought of Bahytzhan and his bug-bitten face. Now he would grow up German instead of American—his whole life changed because of a choice that took place in a single minute.

Jaden held some bread close to his chest without

particularly feeling like eating it. Far away, he saw a shepherd and some sheep strolling in the steppe under the full moon. The wind was blowing hard, and even as high up as Jaden was, he could feel occasional pings on his face from the dust. Finally he had to close the window. Then tears fell down his face as he squeezed the bread to his chest. He didn't know exactly why he was crying. What was he doing here, how did he get here? How? So he was born. So he lived with his mother. So he was brought to a group home. So he went to America. So now he was here.

He thought about what he'd felt earlier, when he had lost his way. He hadn't expected to feel upset about being lost. Was feeling lost also in a way feeling that he belonged somewhere? That he belonged with Penni and Steve?

Unh, it was like torture to try to figure all this out. Instead he tried to think about electricity. Before anyone really understood electricity, there'd been entertainers who'd performed tricks with electricity for the amusement of the public. Like, they could make audience members hold hands and then discharge electricity to one person, which would make everyone in the chain jump at the same time.

Jaden knew that even today, there were many things about electricity that people didn't know. He thought electricity held the secrets of the universe. The electricity in the bodies of the living was always moving and shifting. Every thought people had was electric. When humans understood electricity, they would be immortal.

But even that couldn't distract him just now. Jaden thought of his mother and how he couldn't remember what she looked like. He could only remember that he'd *once* remembered. And even if he could remember, so what? What good would it do him? Still, he felt that if he ever saw her again, he would have an attachment to her, such as he didn't have with Penni.

If they took Ramazan home, he might possibly never ever know what his mother looked like. Was this fair to Ramazan? Was this right?

Chapter Fourteen

L ate the next morning someone knocked on the door, and Jaden peered out the peephole to see Akerke. He opened the door.

"I have surprise!" Akerke said, as if talking to a young child. "We are going to Syr Darya. Is river that flows through Kyzylorda. Many Americans have enjoyed this river."

Penni was still in her pajamas, but she got dressed, and they all walked down to the alley, where Sam was waiting. When they drove to the street, Jaden saw people everywhere sweeping. And there were a few piles of dead leaves on fire.

"Is cleanup day," Akerke explained without being asked. She added, "It happens once a month. I am very proud of how clean is our city."

The Syr Darya was not very wide and was pretty tame, flowing slowly. Dry grass and grayish-green foliage lined the area next to it. The wind blew as hard as it had the day before.

Jaden thought the river area was beautiful in a barren, dilapidated, run-down sort of way. The path alongside the river might have been nice years earlier. In some sections the tiles were intact and easy to walk on. In others, whole sections of tile were missing. There was broken glass all over. Many of the benches they first came across were missing their boards. But farther out the benches were in better shape. Lots of crows were picking at sunflower seed shells that people must have dropped while sitting here.

They continued on until the sidewalk ended and there was only a dirt path in front of them.

"Oh, there!" Akerke cried out. "A camel! They come near the river. This is my surprise for you."

The camel was idly nosing through some grass but lifted his head as they moved toward it. As they got closer, the camel stared right at Jaden, and for a paranoid moment Jaden thought it might be the same camel who'd chased him the day before.

"I appreciate camels, but I do not love them," Sam said glumly. "But Akerke has discovered that the Americans feel love for camels. So we bring you here." His cell phone rang, and he took it out of his pocket. He said something in Russian, and then another phone rang from another pocket. He took out a second phone, saying only, "I am working" in English before hanging up. Then he said, "I am working" into the first phone and put both phones into his pockets.

Akerke was saying, "'Camel' comes from Arabic word for 'beauty.'"

Sam added, "The Americans see camel's thick eyelashes, and this they think is beautiful. I too see beauty in the camels, but only in how they are built to survive in desert. This is beautiful. Eyelashes are not what is beautiful." He shrugged. "But I rarely say so to the Americans. They want to believe it is eyelashes which make camels beautiful, so this I let them think. I only tell you now because Jaden seems like boy who wants to know truth."

"The eyelashes *are* beautiful," Penni said.

Sam shrugged like, *What did I tell you?*

The camel made a spitting noise, and a big hunk of pink skin was extruded from its mouth, just hanging there. "Is that his tongue?" Jaden asked.

"Is the lining of his mouth!" Akerke said excitedly. "You are lucky. Most Americans do not get to see this. They can spit out lining of their mouth! And lining of mouth is so tough that they may eat thorns and do not feel pain." She paused, then said, "The camel lives for forty years. Their humps store fat, not water as many believe." She acted very pleased and proud, as if this camel were a personal pet she was showing off.

Then, just like the other camel Jaden had kind of met, this one became extremely interested in him. It walked forward, then pushed its nose at Jaden's left ear. He stepped back, and it stepped forward and nosed him again, almost pushing him over. Then Jaden trotted a few steps away, but the camel didn't follow and instead stood there watching him. "Camels don't like me," Jaden said a little worriedly.

"Or perhaps this camel likes you. It is hard to say which way it feels," Sam said. "Who are we to say what this camel does or does not like, eh?"

But it was time to head back so they could make it to their bonding session. Sam's limping grew worse as they walked. Jaden slowed down a bit so that Sam wouldn't be left behind so much. "Jaden, did you like the river?" asked Akerke.

"Yeah, it was kind of beat up," Jaden answered. "But I liked that."

"What is this?" Sam said.

"It was kind of old and falling apart," Jaden explained.

"Ah, it is not new," Sam said. "Americans are interested in what is new."

"You have a lot of opinions about Americans," Jaden replied.

"What is this? I have same number of opinions as anyone!"

Jaden decided to let it go.

When they arrived for bonding, the toddlers were outside. The boy from the day before recognized Jaden and chopped at the air with his arms, grinning. He clumsily loped to Jaden even as the caretaker called to him. It sounded like his name was Dimash.

"Mom, I'm going to stay outside for a while. I'll be right there. This is the kid I was talking about. His name is Dimash."

Steve and Penni looked at Dimash, then at each other. Steve said, "But, Jaden, you need to bond with our baby. He's going to be your brother."

"I know, Dad. I'll be right in. I want to talk to Dimash here for *one* minute—no, two—maybe five."

Steve and Penni looked at each other again, and Steve finally said, "Okay, but just for a minute. I expect to see you inside in a minute. As in *one* minute."

When the adults went inside, Dimash grunted. "Unh, unh!" Then he stood very still, frowned a bit, and gazed into the air. *"Kak dyela,"* he cried out, then laughed. He twirled around, laughing and saying, *"Kak dyela, kak dyela."*

Jaden knew that meant "How're things?" He'd read that in a Russian phrase book. *"Kak dyela,"* he said back.

Dimash laughed and flapped his arms. He was probably around four years old, and Jaden knew that kids aged out of the baby house when they turned four or five. Penni had told him that in America.

Jaden said, "Whassup, dude?"

Dimash smiled.

"Hey, I got something for you." Jaden reached into his pocket and pulled out a bag of M&M's he'd brought from the States. He handed an M&M to Dimash.

Dimash studied it and smiled widely. "It's candy," Jaden said. "Candy." He took out an M&M for himself and put it in his mouth. "Mmmmm, this is good. Go on, eat it."

Dimash didn't do anything, so Jaden took out another M&M and placed it right into the boy's mouth.

Dimash opened his eyes wide and shook his head as if an electric jolt had passed through him. "Unh!"

"That's called 'candy.'"

Suddenly the other kids ran at Jaden and held out their hands. The caretaker rushed over and tried to grab Dimash, but he ran away. She chased after him and caught him, scolding him in Russian as he screamed. Then she started yelling at Jaden. When she didn't stop, he put his hands in his pockets and decided to wander inside.

The place seemed deserted and smelled less strongly of bleach than it had the day before. He heard chirping from a bird. He checked the director's office, but it was empty. *"Kak dyela,"* he said to himself. Then, very faintly, he heard singing, or imagined he did. He knew it was Penni because she was singing "What a Wonderful World."

He leaned into a doorway and saw Penni, Steve, Ramazan, and two other couples with babies. He wondered where the toddlers met with *their* future parents. The walls were painted with two big, bright murals of forest scenes. There was a long couch in a big open space with a rug on the parquet floor. Someone—maybe an interpreter—was sitting idly on a bench at a piano. A big sky-blue Kazakh flag hung behind the piano.

Jaden stepped to the window and saw that the toddlers were still outside, playing in the courtyard.

He turned back around and watched the parents and babies interacting. The other grown-ups were talking in what Jaden thought might be German. What was this place anyway? This place where parents converged and babies were taken from their homeland to live half a world away?

Steve called out, "Come on over here, Jaden. Let's be a family."

Jaden sauntered over to where Penni and Steve were sitting on the floor next to Ramazan. Ramazan stared into space. What was up with that? Jaden squatted on the floor next to the baby. "Whassup, buddy?" Ramazan didn't respond. "Hey, I got something for you." He reached into his pocket and pulled out the bag of M&M's.

"Don't give him that," Steve hissed, looking around like they'd get in trouble.

"I'm just going to rub it on his tongue," Jaden replied. And before Steve could say another word, Jaden shook out a candy and rubbed it on Ramazan's tongue. The baby didn't respond at all. Jaden rubbed the candy on Ramazan's tongue again, and again Ramazan didn't respond.

"Let me try!" Penni said eagerly. She rubbed the candy on the baby's tongue, and once again he didn't respond.

Jaden leaned over Ramazan and said, "Sugar." He held up the candy. "Shhhhhooooger."

"The adoption agency said we're only supposed to feed them baby food," Steve said urgently.

Jaden flicked the same piece into the air, caught it in his mouth, and went to sit on a couch. He already understood that baby. That baby didn't want anything, didn't feel anything, didn't even taste candy on his tongue. Jaden lifted up his M&M's bag and poured all the rest of the candies into his own mouth. Should he chew or should he suck? He decided to chew, mashing his teeth into the chocolate. Oh man, oh man, oh man.

Chapter Fifteen

It was stifling in the bonding room. Though it was daytime, the sky was overcast and someone had switched on the overhead light. The equivalent of a seventy-five-watt lightbulb, Jaden guessed. In terms of electricity consumption, the United States was second in the world behind China. Kazakhstan was thirty-second, Romania forty-fifth. He'd looked it up.

He watched one couple holding up cards with pictures and then telling their baby what each picture was, trying to get her to repeat after them. The mother kept kind of studying Penni and Steve, and Jaden wondered if that was the couple who'd wanted to adopt Ramazan. Their baby was a frowner, and very small. Since babies supposedly didn't go on the adoption register for six months, and then there was probably paperwork involved, he figured the youngest babies up for adoption were probably in the eight-month range. But the baby looked smaller than Jaden's cousin had looked at that age.

Jaden finished his candy and plopped down on the floor cross-legged like Steve and Penni were. The baby lay in the middle, on his stomach now as Penni pushed over one of those toys that popped back up whenever you pushed it down. Ramazan was not interested.

Penni and Steve tried to get him to crawl by moving a few feet away and calling to him. He hardly noticed them. Instead he rolled over and over while Steve and Penni followed him. He rolled all the way across the floor and stopped at the wall. Steve and

Penni were delighted. Even Jaden thought it was pretty cute.

Jaden thought he was going to cry then—at what, he didn't know. Then he thought it might be jealousy. He was jealous of this baby. This baby wasn't going to start fires. This baby wouldn't need a thousand shrinks. Probably. Jaden got up and stomped out of the room. He slammed the door behind him, then kicked the wall twice.

Steve opened the door just as a baby house caretaker started running toward him. She paused, as if maybe she was scared. Steve grabbed Jaden by the upper arm. "I want you to stop this behavior right now. Come on, I'm taking you down to the car. You can remain there if you can't participate."

Jaden walked ahead of Steve, straight to the car, without a word spoken between them. He slipped into the seat next to Sam and slammed the door. Steve glared at him, then strode swiftly back to the baby house. Jaden leaned against the headrest and said, "I don't even want a brother. I'm going to have some bad days when we get home."

"How can you have bad days?" asked Sam. "How old are you? A child knows nothing about bad days. Let me tell you, I know bad days."

That made Jaden curious about Sam. "You're not a very happy man, are you?"

"Happy! Of course I am happy. Eh? What makes you say I am not happy?"

"'Cause you keep complaining."

"You are hooligan, you try to make trouble." Sam paused, then continued. "Ah ha ha ha, I am right, I see it in your eyes. A hooligan!"

"I don't even know what a hooligan is."

"What do you mean? How can you not know what you are? You make no sense. But never mind. Come now, let's be friends. We will be spending many time together for next few weeks. Let's not argue. You are hooligan, but I am open-minded man."

Jaden assessed Sam. He wasn't a bad sort. Maybe he was a little emotional, and maybe he complained a lot, but like he said, they would be spending a lot of time together in the coming weeks. Jaden nodded once at Sam, then held out his fist for Sam to bump.

"What is this, you want to punch me?"

Jaden laughed. He liked this man. "In America when two guys want to say 'good job' or 'way to go' or 'okay, fine,' they touch each other's fists. It's called a 'fist bump.'"

"I see." Sam solemnly put out his fist, which Jaden tapped with his own. Then they both put their fists down. Sam nodded his head. "It is good thing, this fist bump. Between two men. Yes, it is good."

"Cool."

Sam leaned back importantly, and then, as if he was trying to be modest but just couldn't, he said, "I know this word 'cool.' Huh? You said that to test me, didn't you? I have been to America, I know this word. Eh? Eh? I am right, that is why you don't answer."

Jaden laughed.

"Yes, I understand you," Sam said. "You would not know it by seeing me, but I know many things. I was born already knowing a lot. Ask my mother, and she will tell you this is true."

Jaden suddenly wanted more candy, or any kind of food. Sometimes the need for food simply overwhelmed him. "Do you have any candy?"

"I am not the candy man," Sam replied. He paused. "I must smoke now," he said earnestly. "I know to Americans it is bad habit, but I cannot stop. I have accepted this." He got out of the car and lit a cigarette.

Jaden looked out the window toward the baby house. He wondered if he could find out what schedule the toddlers were on. He was worried about this Dimash. He was way too skinny. What would become of these toddlers? There was no life if you didn't have a family. Jaden knew this because he didn't have a family, not really. That was why his life was worthless.

Jaden watched Sam smoke and wished he were

Sam. Sam had the confidence of a man with a family. Jaden saw this self-assurance frequently in kids at school. Sometimes it was mean. Like, some of the mean kids felt completely confident and were snobby to others who maybe felt unsure of themselves. That was why Jaden acted confident at school. That and the fact that he really was confident about some things, like namely that he understood the world better than those snot-heads in their trendy clothes ever would. They didn't even realize that they were made of snot.

Jaden closed his eyes and slept. . . .

"Jaden!" It was Steve, back at the car. "Wake up. Don't sleep now or you won't be able to sleep tonight. We need to get on a Kazakh schedule. Please. We've talked about this. Don't make trouble in every single thing you do. I don't want to battle you now when we're having such a titanic experience in our lives. We are experiencing a revolution in our very existence."

Jaden had no idea why Steve was in a bad mood,

then remembered kicking the wall. Still, sometimes he wondered whether every single person
he ever talked to for the rest of his life would think
that he tried to make trouble. All he wanted was
the opposite of trouble. He wanted easy street.
Why was that so much to ask? After all, he was
an American now. Where was the easy street he'd
been told he would find?

Sam was already back in the car, and Penni, Steve,
and Akerke got in. "Is nice baby, your baby," Akerke
said happily.

There was a pause, and then Penni said, "Yes." But
Jaden could hear stress in her voice.

Sam screeched out of the parking area. At the road,
Jaden bumped upward as Sam sped over a pothole.

"Is there a law against driving slow?" Jaden asked.

"No, is no law," Akerke piped up.

"I believe he was being sarcastic," Steve said.
"'Sarcastic' means he didn't ask the question seriously."

"A joke?" Akerke asked.

"No, no, not a joke. Let's see, how can I put it?"

Jaden yawned. If there was one thing Steve liked to do, it was think about words.

"Do you know what 'mocking' means? But no, he wasn't trying to mock. He was highlighting the fact that Sam was driving too fast, but the way he did it was to say the opposite of what he really meant."

"What's this?" Sam asked passionately. "You question my driving? You would want me to drive like I am ninety years old when I am only sixty-seven? I cannot do such a thing until I am ninety! It would not be possible."

Jaden studied Sam's profile. "You're a little sensitive."

"I know this word. I am sensitive like many intelligent people. Ah, you didn't expect me to say that, did you?"

Jaden laughed. "You're funny. I like you."

Sam chortled. "Eh? You make me laugh. That is not so easy to do."

"So how did the bonding go?" Jaden asked.

There was a pause, then Penni said, "It was nice."

"Good, good, good!" said Akerke.

Steve groaned. "Ahhh, I already miss my motorcycle. I need to de-stress." Jaden agreed but didn't say so.

They came to a red light and screeched to a stop. There was the sound of screeching behind them and then another screech that ended with the sound of metal hitting metal.

Jaden watched a pack of dogs chasing after a cat on the street. The dogs caught up and immediately fell upon the cat, surrounding it. "Did you see that?" Jaden said. "That cat—there's a cat in the middle of all those dogs."

Nobody answered. Jaden kept watching as they drove away, but he didn't see the cat again. He felt a stab of sadness.

When they got back to their apartment, Akerke said, "Very good. Sam will come for you tomorrow."

Back in the apartment, Penni fell onto the couch and said, "I don't know. I just don't know. He's so vacant. Do you think there's something wrong with him?"

"We need to take him to an American doctor," Steve said. "Do you think there is one in Kyzylorda?"

"No, remember that lady who adopted here said you can't take the baby anywhere until after the waiting period, when he's completely ours?" Penni said, her forehead bunched up with worry.

She had a crazy expression, like she wanted to scream. Steve sat beside her.

"For him, it's like we aren't even there," Steve said.

Jaden roused himself. "One of the babies at the Almaty airport was the same way."

Penni said eagerly, "Really? Do you think that's normal?"

Jaden shrugged. "I'm just saying."

Penni fell into Steve's arms, sobbing. Steve held her tightly. Jaden had never seen them exactly like this, but he realized there must have been many days and nights she sobbed in Steve's arms when Jaden was misbehaving. He watched them curiously.

"Honey," Steve was saying. "It's just all the pressure. We're under pressure to bond with this baby instead of the one we'd expected. I think that's all it is. We're under a lot of pressure to begin to love Ramazan."

After four years with Penni and Steve, Jaden still didn't know what kind of promises their adoption agency had made to them about him. But he knew they'd expected him to be the center of their lives, and in fact, now that he thought about it, he *was* their center—until this new adoption started. But of course he wasn't the center they'd expected.

"You know, you weren't what I expected either!" he blurted out angrily.

"What, hon?" said Penni, her face confused and tearstained. She pulled away from Steve.

"You were disappointed with me. That's why you're adopting another boy. And now you're disappointed with *him*."

"Jaden, Jaden. We're not disappointed with him," Steve said. "We're just worried. We don't know what's normal. We don't think we can handle a special-needs child, that's all."

"Because you have me, right? Be honest."

"Jaden," Penni said, "I am not even slightly disappointed in you. We are absolutely not talking about you. We're thinking about the totality of our family. What makes sense in terms of our being a family?"

"You want it to be easy."

"That's not it. It's just, it's just . . . We don't want it to be any harder than necessary."

Jaden swung an arm, deliberately knocking a floor lamp on its side. One doctor had said he had a knack for drama, and ever since then, whenever he lost his temper, he could step outside his body and view himself being dramatic.

He went into his bedroom and pushed a chest against the door. In a moment Penni knocked. "Jaden?"

He heard Steve say, "He's being dramatic. He *wants* you to come after him. Don't let him control you."

"I have to," she said. "Dr. Wilder said he's in pain."
She knocked again.

Jaden leaned against the chest, because Penni
was stronger than you might think. Sometimes his
whole world was just so crazy. Like, here he was
in Kazakhstan pushing against a chest that was
pushed against the door, and Penni, his supposed
mother, was on the other side trying to get in. Why
was all this happening to him? Why wasn't he a
normal kid? Or did things like this go on in other
kids' lives too?

Chapter Sixteen

After a while Penni went away, so Jaden sat at his window to watch for more shepherds. He didn't see any, and he became aware that he was hungry. He didn't want to leave his room. He liked how separate from the whole world he felt in here. Sometimes the only thing that you had to protect yourself was a closed door between you and the rest of the world. He hadn't had that in Romania. He loved doors!

He sat on the floor next to his luggage and opened it up, grabbing one of the Ziploc bags of granola. Ziploc, that was another thing that was kind of cool about America. In Romania he'd kept all his things in an old Ziploc that originally came from who knew where. He'd found it on a street. After it was decided he'd be adopted by Penni and Steve, they sent him a hand-held Nintendo. Once the Nintendo ran out of power, there was nowhere for him to recharge it because, though he'd been sent an adapter, the house he was staying at didn't have electricity. But he'd put it in his Ziploc along with a broken rock he'd found with crystals inside. As a matter of fact, he had that rock in his luggage. He'd originally thought it was a diamond.

He shoveled granola into his mouth. For some reason he was shivering. It wasn't cold. After a while he got thirsty. But he sat there eating an entire bag of granola. Then he lay on the floor next to his suitcase. Penni and then Steve knocked at some point, but they didn't try to push the door open. At home they'd once taken off the door to his room because he kept barricading himself in there. That was when he'd burned his teddy bear's face.

When it had been dark for a long time, he pushed the chest aside and stepped outside his room. Penni and Steve seemed to be asleep. He used the bathroom, drank water that Penni and Steve had bought, then returned to his room and pushed the chest against the door. He was incredibly tired but couldn't fall asleep. He lay on the floor, trembling again, his teeth chattering though it wasn't cold. He was so screwed up. He knew this in his head, but he didn't know what to do about it.

In a while he got up and paced back and forth around his dark room, switched the light on and off for a while, and paced some more. Someone pounded on the floor. His footsteps must have been bothering the people who lived below. A couple of hours passed, but Jaden still couldn't fall asleep. He sat at the chair in front of the window. The moon was sinking on the horizon. The steppe was lonely and beautiful, and he couldn't take his eyes from it. Loneliness flooded his whole body like it was a physical sensation, not merely a feeling. Like it was a liquid that had replaced his blood and flowed inside his veins as his heart pumped it through. He wasn't even Jaden anymore; he was loneliness. He wanted to take a picture of all this loneliness: a picture of the steppes, of his room, of himself, but he remembered his phone wasn't charged. How annoying. They'd brought adapters, so he plugged in his phone.

It was getting light when he finally lay in his bed and fell asleep. When he awoke, it was to the sound of Penni and Steve pushing open the door. He watched as the chest was pushed forward. When they got in, Penni and Steve looked exasperated.

"What are we going to do with you, young man?" Steve said, but he didn't seem to want an answer. "Come on, let's go eat."

Jaden didn't bother to change clothes, and they all left the apartment. Apparently, Akerke had told Penni and Steve where some restaurants were. They walked just a few minutes and came to an area full of shops, kiosks, and restaurants.

Steve said, "What do you think, Jaden?"

Jaden lifted his nose into the air the way he some-times saw dogs do. He had an incredible sense of smell. At home if Penni or Steve thought they smelled something odd, they would ask him for his thoughts about it. He led them to a kiosk that was giving off the smell of good bread. "Here," he said.

There was a small crowd around the kiosk. "Where do you suppose the end of the line is?" asked Penni.

They stood in back of what might have been the end of the line. But people kept butting in front of them. "There is no line," Jaden said. He pushed his way in. Somebody said something sharply to him in Russian, but he didn't budge. And whenever anyone tried to butt in, he held his ground.

When Jaden reached the front of the counter, saliva filled his mouth at the thought of biting into this delicious-smelling bread. He took out his tenge and bought three loaves of bread. Then Penni called out, "Don't forget some meat!" So he pushed his way back to the counter and bought some meat. Then, at a small wooden store, they bought cucumbers, tomatoes, and yogurt, which came in a plastic bag.

They decided to eat at home, but Jaden tore off hunks of bread and ate as they strolled. Somebody yelled something at him as he was devouring the bread, but he didn't care what anybody thought. In fact, the great thing about being here was that it seemed like nothing mattered, even though to Penni and Steve, *everything* probably mattered.

When they got back to their apartment, Jaden swore he could smell those tomatoes. He bit into one like it was an apple, and it tasted better than any apple he'd ever eaten. Sweet and juicy and tangy— perfection. He loved perfection when it came to food.

Later they waited in the alley for Akerke and Sam to pick them up. Sam was in a jovial mood. "How are my favorite Americans?" Sam asked. "Eh?"

"There's some good food in Kazakhstan," Jaden said.

"If it is good food you want, you need to go to Turkey. I am from Turkey, so this I know. There is no better rice than pilav. You may go all over world, and you will not taste better rice."

This interested Jaden quite a lot. "Rice? What do you mean? How can it be that good? It has no taste."

"What! Are you mad? Rice is known all over world as perfect food."

"I love perfect food," Jaden replied. "Today I ate a tomato that was perfect."

"Pahhh! I will have my wife make for you some *ezme*. It is salad with tomatoes. You will realize that until you taste that salad, you have never tasted a tomato."

Jaden liked this man! He liked him a lot.

When they arrived at the baby house, the toddlers were out. The boy Dimash spotted Jaden immediately and kind of ran over, or at least tried to, but he was too uncoordinated. Jaden took out his phone and snapped a photo of Dimash. The boy stopped himself by loping right into Jaden.

"Come on," Steve said.

"Dad, Mom, this is Dimash. We could adopt him."

Penni knelt down in front of Dimash. "Hello," she said, rubbing his cheek with her hand. He leaned away from her. "He's very shy."

"Not with me," Jaden bragged. "I'm already his best friend."

"We must go now for bonding," Akerke reminded them.

But Penni wasn't finished saying hello. "What beautiful hair he has. So thick and shiny."

"Remember when you told me that your cousin had an old soul?" Jaden asked. "That's the way he is, I'm sure of it."

Penni softly touched Dimash's face. This time he didn't pull away. "Yes, I see it," she said.

"We must go," Akerke repeated.

Penni stood up.

"I'll be right there," Jaden said. He motioned to Dimash. "Come here, I'm going to teach you how to walk. You gotta walk like you don't care."

Steve hesitated, but Jaden saw Penni take his hand and lead him away. Jaden tilted his head a little and sauntered down the courtyard. "Like that, man. You gotta be cool or nobody will take you seriously."

Dimash laughed like Jaden had said something very funny. "Come on," Jaden said. "I'm serious. Be cool." He walked again, and Dimash ran right into him, then laughed more. "What am I going to do with you? You gotta learn some of this, or— or you're gonna have one bad life. You gotta have people respect how chill you are."

Dimash eagerly nodded his head over and over. At first Jaden thought he nodded because he understood, but then Dimash smiled slightly and turned around in a circle several times. The caretaker was watching them. Jaden ignored her, and soon she was busy with the other toddlers.

"Hey, look, do you know how to clap?" Jaden clapped his hands. Dimash laughed. Jaden stomped a foot. Dimash laughed. Jaden mussed up his own hair. Dimash laughed. "Say something, Dimash. Why don't you talk?"

Akerke came out and said, "Jaden, I know you are busy, but you need to come in. Baby house director says you must bond with Ramazan or she will not approve the adoption."

"Let her say it, that's not my problem."

"Jaden, please, I beg you. She would like the whole family bonding."

"I'll come if you can find out why this boy doesn't talk more."

Akerke frowned at Jaden, then called out to a caretaker and had an exchange of words. Then Akerke said, "This boy is not well. I don't know the words to explain. He cannot talk well—all he says is *'kak dyela.'* He cannot think well. He cannot move well. He is not well and will never be well. Is a problem in his nerves and his brain. He also has problems in his stomach. He may not live for long, which is a blessing."

"Do you think we could adopt him?"

"Your parents have said they do not want a special-needs baby." But then Akerke's eyes grew

163

soft, even sympathetic. "Jaden, this boy will never be able to talk more. I know is sad story, but is *his* story."

Jaden stared at Dimash for a moment. "I gotta go, but maybe we can adopt you. I'll ask my parents."

He walked off, and Dimash barreled into him from behind. Jaden laughed, which made Dimash laugh. "Later, I'll be back, I promise."

When he got to the bonding room, Steve was kneeling down with the baby in his arms, then standing up and saying, "Wheee." He did this over and over. The baby didn't make any sign that he knew he was being lifted or held. He wasn't even making eye contact with anyone.

Jaden sat on the couch and chewed on his nails. Steve placed Ramazan on his stomach, and then Penni and Steve sat cross-legged in front of him. Ramazan was staring between them. At that moment Jaden felt absolutely nothing toward Ramazan. Not jealousy, not interest, just nothing. Penni said, "Jaden, come here in case the director comes in. She specifically said that you should be bonding."

The door opened and there she was—the baby house director.

"Jaden, please!" Penni begged in a low voice. The baby house director frowned.

Jaden walked over and leaned toward Ramazan. "Hey, guy, I'm your brother." And as luck would have it, for the first time, the baby made eye contact with Jaden. Jaden felt a jolt, like the baby had sent some electricity his way. "I know," he said to Ramazan, unsure what he meant by that.

"He looked at you!" Penni said.

"Jaden, tickle him or something," Steve said. "We need to get through to this baby."

Jaden tickled the baby's stomach, but he didn't respond. The moment was over.

The director said something sharply, but since for some reason Akerke wasn't there right then, nobody had any idea what the director was saying. She regarded the whole room and then said angrily, "Because! Because!" That made no sense. She swept out of the room like a queen in a movie Jaden had seen once. He couldn't remember which. For a while after he'd gotten to America, Jaden couldn't get enough of movies. *Star Wars* had been his favorite at one point. Films were light shows, people made of light moving around on a screen in a dark room. But he didn't really like them anymore. All those aliens, fights, shootings, and love stories began to blend together. It was the same movie over and over. Basically, someone who's an underdog triumphs. What did that have to do with real life? Nothing, that's what.

Chapter Seventeen

When their two-hour bonding period ended, they returned to the car. Sam had a cigarette in his hand, a cigarette behind his ear, and a cigarette in his mouth. Jaden liked this crazy guy.

"Hey," Jaden said to Sam.

"This I know. There is a life after this one."

"What does that have to do with anything?" Jaden asked.

"I have not said it had to do with anything."

"True."

Sam stepped on his cigarette butt and picked it up, wrapping it in a cloth from his pocket that was filled with cigarette butts. Then he got into the car, turned on the ignition, and backed up like an insane person.

"Excuse me, Sam!" Steve said. "I don't want to die in a car."

"I do not want to die in car either. This we have in common."

Jaden watched a glass eye swinging from the rearview mirror as Sam pulled into the road. He'd seen that same eye hanging at the kiosk where they'd bought bread. "What is that eye?" he asked Sam.

"It is eye that wards off evil eye that some evil people give to you. If someone breaks my windshield, it is not their fault. It is fault of evil person who has given my windshield evil eye. You must be ready at all times for this eye; therefore you must have glass eye everywhere you go to protect yourself."

"Cool." Jaden's mind drifted to bread. Someday he would like to live in a house of bread.

Penni suddenly groaned. "Oooooh." Next she squeezed her forehead with her hands.

"What is it?" Steve asked in alarm.

"I don't know. I just . . . When Jaden came, I loved him immediately. I know it sounds crazy, but I loved Bahytzhan even though I'd never met him."

The thing Jaden remembered most about his first day in America was that an answering machine had suddenly started talking. He'd been so scared, he'd wet his pants and cried. He'd thought it was some kind of ghost.

"You'll love Ramazan in time," Steve said. "You can't compare different children."

"I know I'll love him! I'm already starting to!" Penni said. "But I'm so worried. I just—just—I don't know if I can handle another—I mean a—I mean what if he's special needs? His legs are so weak. Does it make me a bad person that I don't want a special-needs baby?" She knocked against her head with the heel of her palm. "I'm a bad person!"

"Honey," Steve said. "Pen, it doesn't make sense.

You're upset if you don't love him, and you're upset if you do. You need to inject some logic into this process."

Akerke was sitting up very straight, wearing a slight frown. "Penni, I have seen this before," she said. "You are not the first. Is hard process, this adopting. Is some families it is hard for. One couple—but never mind, every parent is different."

"One couple what?" Jaden asked.

"Is no matter."

"But what were you going to say?" Jaden persisted.

"One couple was very worried about their baby's weak legs."

"What happened?" Jaden asked.

She frowned at him. "All that matters is they loved their baby, and their baby loved them. All was well, as all will be well with your family. Your baby's legs will be fine. They will grow strong. Jaden, I am saying now to your parents."

"It is not my place to speak," said Sam. "For I am only driver, though I know many things. But I cannot stop myself. I must speak. In all my many years most beautiful smile I have seen is smile of my nephew whose legs are very weak. He cannot walk. He has, what do you call it, wheelchair. So I say to you, if your child's legs are weak, you will still see many beautiful smiles from him. This I know from my own experience."

"His legs are not too weak," Akerke said. "I believe all will be well with his legs. I have felt babies with weak legs, and his are strong."

"I am only saying *if* his legs are too weak," Sam said. "I speak from my experience."

"I do not argue with driver," Akerke snapped.

Sam's face went blank, and he bowed his head once. But Jaden could see he was angry inside.

Chapter Eighteen

They spent the next couple of days wandering aimlessly through the city, shopping at the bazaar, and watching the few channels in English on television. The bonding periods were uneventful yet draining. Whenever they tried to feed Ramazan, he would squeal in annoyance and flail his arms, but otherwise he was completely blank. Early one morning Penni and Steve decided to go out for breakfast. Jaden didn't feel like going.

"Promise me you're not leaving the apartment

without us," Penni said. "We don't want you getting lost again."

"I promise," he said easily. Promises were very easy for him to make.

"Well, okay then."

They left the apartment, and Jaden poured himself a bowl of granola, which he ate without milk. Then he watched a show on ESPN about women's billiards, which he ordinarily had no interest in. But he felt desperate to hear English spoken, so the show was a relief to him. It was like getting a drink when you were very thirsty.

Jaden felt good. He had his favorite granola, he had TV, he had an apartment to himself. He heard the door jiggle, and it was already Penni and Steve, back again. Penni immediately said, "Jaden, Sam is coming to pick you up in a few minutes. Akerke called our cell phone and has a special surprise for you. You just have time to eat. We got you some kind of skewered meat and camel's milk."

That didn't sound appetizing, but Jaden followed

Penni into the kitchen and sat at the table.

"What kind of special surprise?" he asked suspiciously.

"Sam is going to take you to go hunting with a friend who hunts with an eagle."

"What's that supposed to mean? 'Hunts with an eagle'?"

"It's exactly what it sounds like. You take the bird out with you, and the bird catches some prey and then comes back to you. It's a Kazakh tradition."

"Are you coming?"

"No, it's a special surprise arranged just for you. It was Sam's idea, to keep you entertained. Akerke is very excited for you."

Jaden picked up the cup of camel's milk and drank. It tasted gamey.

"Camel's milk has all kinds of healing powers," Penni said. "At least that's what the waiter told us, if we understood him correctly."

"So are you excited?" Steve asked. "I wish I were going."

"You can go," Jaden said. "I don't want to."

The cell phone rang. "Hello? Yes, yes, he'll be right there," Steve said. To Jaden, he said, "Sam's here. We'll go down with you."

In the hallway, they moved carefully down the broken steps. Jaden had absolutely no interest in birds. "Why do I have to do this?" he asked.

"Because as soon as Akerke mentioned it, I knew it was a great idea. It's so nice to know Sam was thinking of you. I need to warn you, though, it's an hour away, and then it might take several hours for the eagle to catch prey. But someday you can tell Ramazan all about it!" Penni finished excitedly.

Sam was waiting in his usual place. Penni bent toward the window. "Jaden is very intelligent and loves to learn, so teach him as much as you can, Sam," she said.

"I give you my promise I will teach him well," Sam answered solemnly.

"Mom, I'm going to spend two hours in a car? I don't really want to ride an hour, watch an eagle for who knows how long, and then spend an hour coming back. Can't he teach me about something closer to the city? I'd rather hang with Dimash today if he's outside."

"This is a rare opportunity to observe a Kazakh tradition," Steve said firmly. "This is education the way it's supposed to be, not sitting around all day memorizing data. Do it for your brother."

Jaden didn't want to do anything for his brother. He hardly even knew his brother. Strictly speaking, he didn't even have a brother yet. And even if the baby *was* his brother, he surely couldn't care less if Jaden saw an eagle or not. On the other hand, Dimash would care whether or not he saw Jaden.

But Jaden got into the car with Sam, because he could see that Penni and Steve weren't going to change their minds. That is, he might have been able to manipulate them to change their minds, but he liked to hold back some of his manipulations so that he wasn't doing it too much. A while back he did it all the time, but that backfired because Penni and Steve got so used to him trying to manipulate them that they grew immune to it. So now Jaden had to pick and choose when to be that way.

He didn't say bye, just got in and waited for Sam to start the car.

"Have fun!" Penni called out, but he didn't even glance at her.

Sam turned on the ignition, and they were off. "They have made you to do this trip," Sam said. "But it is not waste of time to see eagle, though you believe it is."

"It's just that I don't really care about eagles. And there's a kid at the baby house I want to hang around with."

They turned onto the street. "You may never come back to Kazakhstan. So you must learn about your brother's country while you are here. Why not? The eagle is powerful bird. I can promise you, you will take some of its power home with you."

Jaden took out his cell phone and snapped a picture of Sam. He had to admit that what Sam was saying interested him. "What kind of power?" he asked.

"The power to become a man."

"I'm going to be a man no matter what. You can't stop from getting older."

"You do not know this, but I am a man with power. The power to be who I must be, though it may irritate my wife. And I want her to have such power too. For instance, she has big nose. If it was smaller, she would be prettier, but she would not be my wife. So when we had much money, she wanted to have surgery to make her nose smaller. We fought about it. Finally she did not have surgery because I did not want that, and she has much respect for me. And I respect her— this is why I did not want her to have smaller nose. Today we will see to it that someday you will have a marriage as good as mine. Many eagles mate for life."

"Why does everyone keep bringing up marriage? I'm twelve years old."

"What? But I am only answering your question! You must not take apart what I say and ask me about each small detail. You must take everything I say together."

Jaden didn't answer; obviously, Sam was in cahoots with Penni, Steve, and Akerke about this eagle business.

When they reached the steppe, the road was empty and the land was yellowed and weedy, with occasional patches of green. Why were some parts green? It went to show that there was a lot of luck in life. Luck was the only thing Jaden could think of that would make one plant green and the one right next to it thirsty and yellow.

After about an hour of driving through the desolate grasslands, Sam announced that they'd arrived. They pulled up to a domed structure, which Jaden knew was a yurt, in the middle of a field. An enclosed area was next to the house, and a horse stood nearby. They got out and walked up to the open door. Inside, several people were sitting on the floor around a low table. There was also an eagle on a perch! Jaden had never seen such a big bird; it scared him. "Kanat!"

Sam called out, going inside. Jaden waited at the door. A small man stood up and embraced Sam.

The two men spoke in Russian. Kanat had a squeaky voice and sounded almost like an animal. Then Sam said, "Here is something which I have learned from this boy. In America, between two men you may touch fists, and this means you are good and all is well. Here, put the hand like this." Sam made his hand into a fist, and Kanat did the same. Sam bumped Kanat's fist and said, "Just touch. It is good thing, no?"

"Sure, sure," Kanat said. He smiled at Jaden. "So you are American. Come sit in my house, it will be wonderful."

Jaden stepped into the house, immediately drawn to the eagle. He moved closer to the bird, still staying a couple of feet back. The eagle's eyes were hidden by a hood on its small head. It sat calmly. Then for some reason it stretched out its wings, which were unbelievably wide—longer than a full-grown man. Jaden froze, his heart pounding from nervousness. The bird definitely looked powerful. It was otherworldly.

"I have named her Kanat, for she is my twin sister," Kanat said. "It is name for boys, but it is right name for her."

"That is very wise," Sam said.

Kanat was pleased and bowed his head.

"And now I may introduce to you Jaden," Sam said. "He would like to see your eagle hunt."

"What, *now*?" Kanat asked.

"Yes, we have come all the way from Kyzylorda city to see this."

"Then of course I will elevate you."

"Elevate?" said Sam. Then he and Kanat spoke to each other in Russian again. Kanat was a thin and darkish Asian man with a short goatee. He didn't look big enough to handle the eagle. Sam and Kanat seemed to finally understand each other, and they both turned to Jaden.

"Yes, yes, power, I see," Kanat squeaked. "So you would like to fly an eagle? It takes many months and sometimes many years to become good eagle handler. It is very long experience, as long as ten years with each eagle."

"Wow," Jaden said. In ten years he would be twenty-two, which was pretty much unimaginable.

"I know an American woman, almost as small as you, who, ah, excelling in eagle handler."

Jaden shrugged.

Kanat said to Sam, "He does not talk much."

"He is sometimes little shy," Sam agreed.

Shy? Jaden had never seen himself like that. If he had something he needed to say, he liked to say it. That wasn't shy.

"Well, I didn't really want to fly one myself," Jaden said. "I thought we only came to watch."

"Yes, it is so," Kanat replied. "You will ride in sidecar with Sam, and I will ride my horse. Then I hope to show you an eagle's power, which, as Sam says, you have driven far to see." Kanat put on a huge thick glove, then went to the perch and detached what looked like two leather strings holding the eagle down. He placed his gloved hand under the eagle, which climbed onto the glove. Next Kanat attached the strings to his glove. Sam and Jaden followed Kanat out, the eagle still hooded. With no word spoken, a woman came outside with them and saddled the horse.

Kanat expertly climbed the horse while holding the eagle. The way Kanat treated her, with rapt attention, she seemed like royalty to Jaden. "The sidecar is around the house," Kanat said to Sam.

When they saw the motorcycle with a sidecar, Jaden was struck by how out of place it seemed out here in the wilderness. Sam sat on the motorcycle, Jaden in the sidecar. "You know how to drive this, right?" Jaden asked.

"I say to you modestly that I can drive anything. Put me in rocket, and I will drive you to moon."

The next second the motorcycle was bumping over the field.

After a while they stopped to wait for Kanat. The wind was blowing hard. When Kanat caught up, the two men began to talk excitedly in Russian. They had to shout over the noise from the motorcycle. Then Sam drove on. They rode for a long time, maybe an hour and a half. But Jaden felt at peace in this bleak landscape. It was strange, but he thought it must be like meditating. Two of his doctors had tried to get him to meditate, but he couldn't do it right. But at this moment he felt like he could.

One time Sam had to wait for Kanat, and when he reached them, Kanat said, "Here is good. We stop now." He took the hood off the eagle and undid the leather strings. "She is brilliant eagle. She finds her own prey. I do not do it for her as I must with the many eagles over the years."

Nobody moved. The eagle's eyes darted this way and that, again and again. They all sat doing nothing for about half an hour. But for some reason Jaden didn't feel impatient. Then suddenly the eagle took off into the air, up and up.

"She has seen something!" Kanat cried out.

Jaden jumped up and looked forward and saw nothing. He looked behind himself and to both sides, but he didn't see what the eagle saw. Then in the distance she began speeding unbelievably fast and downward. She swooped toward something that was almost like a bouncing dot on the horizon, and the eagle was not much more than a dot herself. It was hard to tell for sure, but then the dot seemed to make an amazing about-face and headed swiftly in the opposite direction. The eagle didn't change directions quickly enough; the dot was gone. She didn't come back to Kanat, just flew way above them, up and up. Kanat called out, "Meeeeeh, meeeeeh" in a voice so animal-like that Jaden could only deduce that Kanat was part animal. Then the eagle swooped down and landed on his glove. But a few minutes later she took off into the air again, rising upward.

"She has seen another hare!" Kanat cried out. Jaden could see this one. Kanat spurred his horse into a gallop, and Sam drove forward. The eagle fell upon the hare.

When they got to the eagle, she was pecking at a bloody hare that was somehow still alive. Jaden

snapped a picture. It all struck him as simultaneously cruel and exhilarating. He liked the way
she so obviously relished eating raw meat, and he
related to that, but the hare was suffering. Jaden
hopped out of the sidecar to get a closer look. The
eagle glared at him like she wanted to scratch his
face off and have it for dessert. But he didn't take a
step back, because he wanted to see her close up. As
he was watching, the hare died.

"How did she know the first hare was there?"
Jaden asked Kanat.

"Eyes of eagles take up more space than their
brains. She can have sight more than two and a half
kilometers away," Kanat bragged. "She has good
eyes, even for eagle." Jaden tried to work that out in
his head. Maybe somewhere between one and a half
and two miles?

Kanat spoke to the eagle in what sounded like
Kazakh. Then he rehooded her and tied the rabbit
carcass to the horse.

Jaden could feel Kanat's pride radiating out

from him like spokes on a wheel. Sam was nodding appreciatively. Then Sam patted Jaden on the shoulder. "Eagle is built to be predator," Sam said. "There is nothing else that matters to eagle when she chases hare. It is drive for prey that makes her so fast. Someday you must find out what makes you fast, do you see?"

Fast? Jaden watched as Kanat climbed back on his horse, the eagle on his glove. There was a forked post attached to the saddle, and Kanat rested his gloved arm in the fork. It had all gone so quickly, Jaden hadn't had time to process everything. What did Sam mean by "fast"? He didn't know what kind of power he might have gained, though the eagle was very impressive. Even so, he felt a pang of sadness for the bloody hare.

"It's sad for the hare," Jaden said.

"Yes, sure," Kanat answered. "A hare is very wonderful. I have much respect for prey." He became sorrowful momentarily, and then the pride filled his face again. "Often you don't catch something so soon. Sometimes it takes many hours. But she wanted to put on show for you. She is not as quick as some eagles, and many times she cannot catch hares because a hare has much of speed."

"How come you use a girl eagle?" Jaden asked.

"The females are bigger and perhaps braver. She once took down a wolf. Many do not believe she did this, but it is true. Kanat is best eagle I ever knew."

The eagle was sitting peacefully on Kanat's gloved arm. Jaden stepped closer and then closer until he was right next to her. Her feet were as long as his own feet. "The talons are very strong," Kanat said. "The beak as well."

"Come now, Jaden," said Sam. "I will get you back to your parents. Maybe you will have time to see your friend at baby house. I did not know things would go so well. I am very pleased."

They rode back to Kanat's house, but this time Jaden didn't feel like he was meditating. It was hard to meditate when you've just seen a giant bird swooping through the sky. It made him feel kind of wired, then sad for the hare, then wired again. They arrived at the yurt before Kanat. Jaden got up, closed his eyes, and concentrated. But he didn't feel more powerful. "I don't feel any extra power," he said.

"Maybe you will feel it, and maybe you will not. But it will be inside you, I promise you this."

When Kanat got home, he placed the hooded eagle on the perch in an outside enclosure. "The hood keeps them calm," Kanat said.

What would it be like for such a bird to be cooped up all day? "Is she happy?" Jaden asked.

"Happy!" Kanat said. "It is my usefulness to see to it that she is happy!" To Sam, he said, "You will come in for drink? I have vodka."

Sam looked tempted, but then his face fell. "I have promised my wife I would never drink when I must drive, and I do not like to lie to my wife. But next time I will stay all day. Save your vodka for me."

"Sure, sure," Kanat said.

"Thank you," Jaden said. "Great eagle."

"Sure, sure."

Jaden got into the car with Sam. As he started the car, Sam said, "Do not lie to your wife. Even if she does not find out, you will be mistaken to lie to her. Listen to me—I am teaching you well, as I promised your mother."

"I think she meant to teach me about eagles."

"The eagle may teach you herself. It is my duty to teach you about your wife. This is one lesson of today."

After that, Sam didn't talk for most of the way back, during which time he drove like a madman, as usual.

Then he asked, "Jaden, what have you thought your power will be?"

"I have no idea."

"You will find something that makes you fly, and then your life will be settled. What is it you thought of the eagle?"

"I'm not sure. She was spectacular, I guess."

"What is this?"

"Spectacular. It means amazing."

"I have shown you an eagle's power, and you have taught me a new word. This is good," Sam said. He held out a fist, and Jaden bumped it with his own.

Chapter Nineteen

They reached the baby house during the last half hour of bonding time. Jaden felt like he'd been in a fantasy world all day, and now he was going back to reality. He felt a little dazed to be in the real world again. Dimash was across the courtyard by an old swing set. He spotted Jaden immediately and started crying out, *"Kak dyela! Kak dyela!"* Jaden stood, waiting and smiling. He enjoyed watching Dimash run toward him. As usual, the boy stopped himself by bumping right into Jaden's stomach, which immediately

brought Jaden back to this world. He was surprised at the lift in his heart when he saw Dimash.
He was a funny little guy. Full Kazakh, no doubt—
he could not have looked more Central Asian.
Beautiful, except you could tell he wasn't right.
His way of running was awkward, and the way
he stood, with one shoulder scrunched down, was
strange. No, the future was not bright for Dimash
if he didn't learn to walk differently. Walking was
important.

Jaden knelt down in front of him. "Dimash, my
man, you need to find the part of yourself inside
that can save you." That was what Dr. Wilder had
said to him once. "What are your brains like in
there? Can you save yourself?"

Dimash gazed at him intently, his shoulder
scrunched, his stance geeky. Jaden pulled the boy's
shoulder up until both sides were even. "Here,
stand like this. Good! Now watch." Jaden walked
evenly, with a little bit of swagger. "That's how you
walk. Come on, walk to me."

Dimash pushed his shoulder down and walked to Jaden even geekier than usual.

"No," Jaden said, patiently but firmly. "When you walk, you must be cool. Then maybe nobody will bother you. Believe me, I've seen what it's like when other kids bully someone. It's bad, okay? I'm not trying to scare you, but I need to educate you." He knew Dimash couldn't understand him. But what if he could sort of understand the concept through some kind of osmosis or exchange of electrons? It was possible. "Watch carefully," he said slowly and seriously.

Jaden sauntered in an exaggerated fashion. Dimash was right behind him, giggling. Jaden sighed. "No, no, no. No. *Nyet.*"

Dimash turned serious.

"Yes, good! This is serious! *Da!*"

Akerke suddenly called out behind them, "Jaden! You are here! You must come to the bonding. Director has said it. She is away but is coming back soon. She should not see you out here when you should be bonding."

Jaden glanced at her, then ruffled Dimash's hair. "Okay, buddy, I'll see you." He bounded up the steps. He felt he might have gotten through to Dimash, just a little. It made him want to jump up a hundred feet!

In the bonding room, not a single thing had changed with Ramazan. The baby's face was blank as a clean chalkboard. Penni walked up and down the room with Ramazan in her arms, her head pressed against his face, his emotionless eyes wide open. A woman Jaden hadn't seen before was playing the piano.

"Back so soon? How was it?" Steve asked.

Penni came over with the baby. "Was it fun?"

Jaden thought that over. "It was another universe, right in the same country as Kyzylorda city."

"What did you learn?" Steve said.

"Not to lie to my wife someday."

Penni and Steve just looked at him. "What does that have to do with eagles?" Steve said.

"Some eagles mate for life, so that taught me, uh,

how to be fast . . . or something like that. It was cool. I'm glad I went."

Jaden sat on the couch, trying to process his information overload. He tried to feel some kind of new power inside himself, but he still couldn't find it. What was the point of new power if you couldn't even feel it? He switched his mind over to the boy. Dimash had been happy to see him, and he'd been happy to see Dimash. They had bonded. This was exactly what the laws wanted kids and families to do. He wanted Dimash for a brother. But how could he make that happen?

Penni was placing Ramazan onto the floor, and then she and Steve sat down a few steps away. "Ramazaaaaan, crawl over heeeere, honey!" Steve said in a talking-to-a-baby voice Jaden had never heard from him.

Jaden sat on the floor next to Penni and Steve. "Mom, Ramazan is a great baby, don't get me wrong. But I think we should adopt Dimash. Someone else may adopt Ramazan, and he'll have

a good life. He's a baby, and you told me everyone wants the babies. But nobody but us will adopt
Dimash. Doesn't that mean the right thing to do
is to adopt him?" Jaden paused, thinking, thinking. . . . Then he had it. "You're always telling me
I should be good inside. You said that's the most
important thing in the world. Wouldn't we be better inside if we adopted Dimash?"

Steve said, "Sometimes you need to make decisions that don't involve taking the most noble action
but rather taking the action that is the most bene-
ficial for you. That isn't always true, but there are
decisions like that, Jaden. But I'm proud of you for
what you've just said."

Jaden was trying to manipulate Penni at the
moment, not Steve. So he ignored Steve.

"Mom?" Jaden said. "Can we adopt him?"

She stared straight ahead, at where Ramazan was
now lying on his back instead of crawling toward
them. She took a big breath and tilted her head at
Jaden, her eyes filling with tears.

"Oh, honey," she said. "I don't think he's right for us. He's a beautiful boy, inside and out, I think, but that doesn't make him the child for us."

Penni fixated on the baby again. "Ramazan, can you crawl to your mommy and daddy?"

Disappointment and worry washed over Jaden. He sat on the couch sideways, so he didn't have to watch Penni and Steve bonding with Ramazan.

When bonding finished that day, they watched TV at their apartment for a while, ate dinner at a café nearby, wandered around for half an hour, and finally went back and watched television again. It was all pretty different from seeing a man hunt with an eagle. Usually when they visited another place, Penni and Steve did touristy things, but here in Kyzylorda they had no interest in being tourists. They had a purpose, and that was to adopt a baby.

Since there weren't many shows in English on their cable, they ended up watching the usual women's billiards in English, the nature channel in English, or tennis matches narrated in Russian.

During commercials they talked about women's billiards, lizards or other animals, and tennis. Lizards now seemed important, even to Jaden. It was just that you kind of glommed on to anything spoken in English, and that made the nature channel take on greater importance.

Finally Jaden went to his room to read about electricity, but for once he wasn't interested in it. He'd brought a great book called *The Spark of Life* that he'd read half of, but at the moment he just couldn't focus. He had too much to process. So he sat at the window, trying to turn himself off. Instead his mind traveled back to the morning. If he were Kazakh, he wouldn't mind being an eagle hunter. The experience had been kind of hypnotic, the way it brought you into the eagle's world. But what did Sam mean about being fast? And what about finding his power?

Penni rapped on the door—he recognized her soft knock—and then the door pushed open just a crack. "Good night, Jaden."

"Good night, Mom."

"Jaden?" He waited. "Do you like the baby?"

"I don't know. He doesn't do much."

"I know. I don't think he's bonding with us. My goal is for us all to love one another before we leave Kazakhstan," she said firmly.

"But, Mom, don't you like Dimash?"

"Very much," she said as she walked into the room.

"I think it's fate that we take him," Jaden said. "It is."

"Oh, but, honey, I don't believe in fate."

"It was fate that you adopted me!" Jaden cried out.

"It wasn't fate, it was chance. But any life that wouldn't have brought you into my family is not one I would have wanted to live," she said, her eyes flashing.

That made Jaden feel something, but what? He didn't know. He didn't understand feelings so well. *Click.* He took a picture of himself, of his expression.

"I don't know if this baby is bonding," Penni continued, sitting on the bed. "I can't get rid of the idea that Bahytzhan was supposed to be our child." Then she gave her head a hard shake and forced a smile. "But Ramazan, he's a wonderful baby. I just want everything to work out. And then there's Dimash. But, honey, it would be so difficult. . . ."

"What?"

"Raising Dimash."

"I would look out for him," Jaden said eagerly. He stood up and took a few steps toward the bed.

"Would you?" Penni asked. "Would you?"

"I said it."

"You've said many things," Penni retorted.

"But, Mom, I mean it."

Steve appeared in the doorway. "Who said what?"

"We were talking about Dimash," Penni explained.

"Dimash," Steve said. "Poor little guy. Beautiful kid, but we can't adopt Dimash."

Jaden pounded his fist against his forehead three times. He knew they hated it when he did that, but he couldn't stop himself.

Steve looked at him coolly, and even Penni

didn't react with worry like she usually did. Still, he could tell that Penni wanted to discuss all this further. But his heart abruptly went cold, and he didn't want to talk anymore. Dr. Wilder had tried making a chart with Jaden about these occasions when his heart went cold. But then it happened so much that they didn't know how to chart it anymore. Dr. Wilder couldn't find any pattern as to when it would happen.

"Good night, you guys."

"Oh, I'm sorry, we're keeping you from your, uh, musings." Penni stood up. "Good night."

Chapter Twenty

Jaden turned off the light and sat at his window to watch the shepherd. There were eleven sheep and what looked like a dog, which occasionally ran in a little circle, as if playing. Shepherds in Kazakhstan were nomads, wandering across the land. Jaden tried to imagine himself in that kind of life, and somehow it made sense to him. No Penni, no Steve, no school, no destination. He took out his phone, and from the opposite side of the room, he snapped a picture of the window.

Then, without changing into his pajamas, he got in bed and fell into a deeply disturbed sleep where he wasn't sure what was real and what wasn't.

For some reason, the toddlers didn't seem to be on an exact schedule. Sometimes when Jaden arrived, Dimash was playing in the courtyard with the toddlers, and sometimes the courtyard was deserted. And then one day when they arrived, there was Dimash, shivering out in the rain, all by himself. He burst into tears when he saw Jaden and ran toward him, throwing his arms around Jaden and sobbing. Jaden hugged him tightly as rain washed over them. As if she were speaking from another world, he heard Penni saying, "Bring him inside, Jaden."

"Which building do the toddlers live in?" he asked.

"Bring him inside this building to the director," Steve said.

They'd just gone inside when one of the caretakers spotted them and grabbed Dimash and yelled at Jaden as if he were somehow responsible.

Jaden yelled back. "What was he doing outside on his own in the rain?"

The caretaker seemed taken aback and pulled Dimash away and outside, probably to where the toddlers lived.

The weather had grown cold so quickly. Jaden worried that the caretakers wouldn't be bringing the toddlers outside anymore because of the weather. How would he get to see Dimash if they were inside?

In the bonding room, Jaden plunked himself down next to Penni and Steve on the floor. A minute later he went to sit on the couch. He felt more worried than he'd ever felt since the day he got to America. Why had Dimash been outside on his own? And why was he crying? He felt his extremities tingling, and he wiggled his fingers and feet. He popped out of his seat and rushed down the steps outside, then picked up speed and threw himself on the ground right in front of Sam's car. He was lying there, enjoying the rain, when he felt Sam's hand on his back.

"What is it? Why were you running? What happened?"

"I don't know," Jaden said. "I don't know. I had to."

"Had to what? Let me see your hands! You're bleeding. Come. Get in car. It is too cold out here."

Jaden examined the blood on his hands and wiped it on his face. When he'd lived in Romania, he'd been told that he would be put out on the streets at age twelve. Even if Dimash never aged out of being institutionalized, he would not have a good life. No, it was impossible for that to happen unless he was adopted. So what if his hands were bleeding? He had more important issues to think about.

Sam helped Jaden to his feet, and they both got into the car. At first they sat quietly. Finally Sam said, "Did you fall on purpose? It did not look like you tripped."

"Yeah, sometimes I do that. I just, I don't know. I wish I could fly, but I can't. It makes me mad."

Sam nodded wisely. "Yes, it makes me mad too,

but that is no reason to wipe blood on your face. We cannot all be the eagle. We must find our own way. That is what the eagle has tried to teach you."

Jaden wondered why he'd never rammed his face on the ground when he did his aggressive running. Maybe one day he would try that. But then he immediately rejected that thought, because he didn't want to harm his handsome face. He laid his head back against the headrest. "It doesn't hurt when I do it," Jaden said. "One of my doctors said I can't feel pain."

"Believe me, you can feel pain. You will learn that you can feel pain. It is a lesson we all must learn. You feel the pain and then you move on."

"Are you bitter?" Jaden asked. He loved the word "bitter." There were so many instances when it was the perfect word to use.

"Yes, I am bitter man. I am happy man, but bitter, too."

"You can't be both at the same time. It's impossible."

"You are telling me that it is impossible for me to

be me?" Sam chuckled. "Believe me, I am me. I am quite possible."

"There's a boy here named Dimash," Jaden abruptly told Sam. "Akerke says he can't talk, think, or move well. There's something wrong with his brains and nerves and his stomach. I can't get my mind off him."

"Yes, I have seen him. Someone gave his mother the evil eye while she was pregnant."

"Is that what happened? Really?"

"I know it is so. The same thing happened to my nephew. A woman gave my sister the evil eye when she was pregnant, and her baby was born with very weak legs, as I mentioned to your parents." Sam paused. "Now let me see your hands."

Jaden held out his hands. There were a lot of scars on his palms, but the blood hid them at the moment. Sam took his hands and studied them. "You are lucky. It is mostly scraped. This cut here is not so good, but not so bad, either. You must promise me you will not do this again."

"I promise," said Jaden easily. Promises were nothing but a form of lying. The problem was, he knew he'd told the truth when he'd basically promised to take care of Dimash. But because of all his lying, Penni might not believe him.

A while later when Penni and Steve got to the car, Penni exclaimed, "Oh, Jaden! What now?" She spoke as if exhausted. She opened the car door and studied Jaden's face. "Did you do your aggressive running?" As an answer, Jaden turned his palms upward for her. She wrapped his hands in the blood-clotting gauze that she carried for just these occasions. "We'll need to clean this when we get back to the apartment. Sit in back with us. Akerke can sit in front."

Jaden sat between Steve and Penni. Even though he was bloody and he knew that bothered them, he could also somehow feel that Steve and Penni were getting more and more relaxed about Ramazan. This would make it harder for him to make a case for Dimash. But he wouldn't give up.

Back in the apartment, Penni tenderly washed his hands with soap, then took out the alcohol wipes she'd also brought for an occasion like this. She was crying, as she sometimes did when she tended to his injuries. But her tears left him cold.

Later, at dinner in a small restaurant, Penni and Steve talked obsessively about their court date, which was in a few days. They worried that the judge might not like them, that the prosecutor would ask them questions they didn't have answers for, and that the final decision would be put off until another day.

That night Jaden stayed up for hours, staring at the dark ceiling.

Chapter Twenty-One

And then, after many days and weeks of not bonding with the baby, their court date arrived. In the courtroom Jaden sat behind Penni and Steve. The prosecutor asked them quite a few questions, but Jaden couldn't make out Akerke's softly spoken translations. It had been quite a scene that morning when Penni had found out that Jaden hadn't brought his suit. She'd screamed at him. It wasn't the first time she'd screamed at him, but she hardly ever did it. Still, he knew there would be times in the future that she would scream again. He'd made her and Steve's lives torture. If the judge knew what he was like, he wouldn't let Steve and Penni adopt a baby. No way would he. Jaden even considered shouting at the judge. That would stop the adoption right then and there. But the judge awarded them Ramazan, and Jaden had a brother . . . almost.

For the next fifteen days after the court date, by Kazakh law, the relatives of the baby would have the opportunity to claim the child if any of them wanted, or the prosecutor could decide to appeal the judge's decision. This was called the "waiting" or "appeal period." If a relative claimed Ramazan, the adoption might be off. Jaden wondered why the waiting period wasn't before the court date. That would make a lot more sense. But whatever—it was *their* country, so they should do whatever they wanted. Penni said that as far as she knew, such a claim or an appeal had never been made, so it was just an exercise. They would continue the bonding during these two weeks, after which they would take custody of Ramazan, but still not be able to bring him home. They would need to fly to the city of Almaty, Kazakhstan, and do paperwork for about ten days. *Then* they could fly home, a family of four.

Jaden got to see Dimash several days in a row. When Dimash first saw him on any particular day, he would flap his arms—he was that excited to see Jaden. Sometimes they just sat together on the steps. On a couple of days Dimash had a hacking cough. Now the caretakers didn't bother them because they realized how happy the boy was to see Jaden. Sometimes Dimash just held on to Jaden's arm and leaned against him as they sat. Dimash would smile to himself as he leaned. The last day Jaden was to see him was the momentous day they would take custody of Ramazan. Jaden brought Dimash chocolate that day. When he gave Dimash a piece, the kid went bonkers. He shook his head, almost like trembling. Then he smiled hugely. Jaden smiled back, and Dimash reached out with both hands to feel Jaden's smile.

"Come on!" Jaden giddily shouted. He broke into a run, pausing to make sure Dimash was following. In a second someone started yelling almost hysterically in back of them. He heard the flip-flop of shoes behind him, from Dimash, and farther back, from the caretaker who was chasing them and shouting.

When they reached the street, Jaden didn't stop. At some point he didn't hear yelling anymore. He laughed as they ran. In fact, Jaden thought he had never felt so happy.

He slowed down to a jog so that Dimash could keep up. They were both laughing. When Dimash got tired, they sat down in an alley next to a garbage bin. They leaned back against the bin to catch their breath. A man in camouflage with a rifle was sitting on a bench next to a door. He stared at them, and for a moment Jaden was scared. Then the man looked away.

Jaden folded Dimash's hand into a fist, then made his own fist and tapped Dimash's curled hand. Dimash's eyes grew serious. Jaden smiled and ruffled the boy's hair. "Great hair, dude."

"*Kak dyela*," Dimash said.

Jaden stared down the alley, and when he next looked, Dimash was playing with a big beetle. The beetle buzzed, and Dimash let out a heartrending scream. Jaden stomped on the beetle with his foot. "It's gone now," he said.

Dimash grabbed him and grunted, "Unh. Unh. Unh."

It was getting dark. Time to get back. Or something. Jaden briefly considered running away. But he knew he couldn't take care of Dimash, couldn't get him food, couldn't get him clothes, couldn't get him shelter.

So they went back. When they reached the baby house, the director, Penni, Steve, Akerke, and two caretakers were standing out there, yelling at one another. Penni was holding Ramazan. She noticed Jaden and Dimash and cried out, "There they are!"

The grown-ups all rushed up as the boys stopped in their tracks. One of the caretakers grabbed

Dimash and pulled him away firmly but not cruelly as he screamed. Then, as he was pulled, he twisted around to see Jaden and desperately reached out. The caretaker was crying for some reason.

Everybody was scolding Jaden at once, in Russian, in Kazakh, in English. Ramazan's eyes were wide open and he looked terrified of all the angry voices. The part of Jaden that could think at that moment took note of the fact that Ramazan was actually showing an emotion.

Jaden bit back tears seeing Dimash pulled away, screaming. This would be his last image of that boy. Jaden's whole body felt limp. In fact, he needed to sit down. So he sat right where he was, listening to Dimash's screams. Somehow Dimash seemed to know that this would be the end of their friendship. Jaden snapped a picture of his last view of Dimash.

"Ohhh," Penni said. She closed her eyes and pressed her fingers to her temples. Then she opened her eyes. "What will become of him?"

"He will be fine," Akerke said. "This is very good

baby house. But now we must leave. Your baby is unhappy."

As Penni watched Dimash being pulled away, she put her fingers over her mouth, as if she wanted to say something but didn't know what.

Steve made Jaden stand up. They all got into the car, Jaden in front with Sam. He felt like he hated Penni and Steve and their whole existence—selling crappy food to schools, answering phones with a smile in their voices.

He closed his eyes as tightly as he could and held his breath, as if he might be able to suffocate himself. Nobody would ever adopt Dimash. Ever.

When Penni, Steve, Akerke, and Ramazan were all in the car, Steve said, his voice low and angry, "I don't need to tell you that you almost ruined this adoption." The baby cried in the background. "The director was threatening to take Ramazan away from us."

Jaden stared out the window. He hated this world.

Miracle of miracles, Sam drove slowly. In fact, he

drove much more slowly than he needed to. The car in back of them honked, then whizzed around them, driving directly into opposing traffic to pass them. That was so insane.

"You're going a little slow," Jaden said listlessly.

"There is baby in car. I must drive the way my deep conscience tells me, for if nothing else I am a deep man. My wife has said it many times. 'Sam, you are a deep man.'"

"Well, it's just that—I don't know, never mind. I'm in no hurry."

Cars continued to pass them, but first the other vehicles would speed up close to their car, then brake hard, then honk repeatedly, and only then whiz around, often right into oncoming traffic.

"A deep man knows right from wrong!" Sam exclaimed.

The baby cried in the car, cried as they climbed up the stairs to their apartment, cried inside their apartment, cried as Penni tried to feed him, and cried off and on all night. All the noise drove Jaden crazy, but at the same time he guessed it was probably a good thing for Ramazan to be emotional.

Jaden lay on the bed for hours, thinking about Dimash and listening to the cries and to the tired voices of Steve and Penni. He wanted to roll into a ball and spin away into a closet and never come out. He didn't want to deal with the world at all. Not. At. All. Or else he'd like being a shepherd, wandering around forever, sleeping beneath the stars. Or he could be an eagle and have total clarity of purpose. "Clarity of purpose" was a Steve phrase. He said you needed "clarity of purpose" to get anywhere in life—in his case, to be a better salesman.

In the morning Jaden lay there listening to the baby's cries. He hadn't known it was possible to cry for so long. Where did all those salty tears come from? He felt sorry for this adopted baby—and he got up and went to the other bedroom, where Penni and Steve were trying futilely to make Ramazan stop crying. "I can hold him for a while," he told them. It surprised even himself when he said that. But it was just that he thought he understood the baby. Penni and Steve looked at him doubtfully but also hopefully. Their hair and clothes were disheveled, and Penni had a dirt streak across her face. She handed Ramazan to him, and Jaden held tight as the baby arched his back to get away. Jaden squeezed him and walked into the living room. Then he circled the border of the living room, his bedroom, and the kitchen. After thirty minutes, he switched directions, just for a change. He made figure eights. He walked. And walked. Hours passed. Penni and Steve were sleeping. His arms were exhausted and his back hurt, and Ramazan didn't stop crying. But Jaden kept going because he understood the baby and knew he was the only one who did.

He tried not to think about Dimash, but he kept thinking about him and about seeing him for the last time. He felt a bitter, cutting love for that kid— and abruptly he stopped in midthought. Is love what he felt? Why, then, would anyone want to feel it?

Jaden began to cry. He cried and cried, but not just for Dimash. He cried also because he suddenly realized how important and powerful he himself was. He was so important that he could ruin his new brother's life. He could ruin Ramazan's life by hating Penni and Steve, and by hating Ramazan. So he cried as he paced the apartment. Because Jaden knew the only way to make sure that this baby had a good life was for him to love the baby, and, more complicatedly, to love Penni and Steve. He could not stop crying—it became full-on sobbing. At some point he could feel Penni behind him, and he turned around. She was there, as he'd known, and so was Steve.

Jaden walked off to his room with the baby, without saying anything to them. He was sorry they'd seen him cry. He hated that.

Another hour passed, and the baby finally fell asleep. Jaden could hear Penni and Steve talking and talking. He laid Ramazan on the pillow and sat on the floor, leaning his back against the bed, tears streaming down his face. He was exhausted. Penni and Steve came into his room. They sat on the floor next to Jaden. Penni said, "We've decided something."

"What?" Jaden asked moodily.

"We've decided we're going to adopt Dimash as well as Ramazan." Then all in a rush she said, "I made a phone call to a social worker back home who I went to school with. We need to go back to America and prepare for Dimash, things like finding a therapist to work with him and joining a support group and reading some books, and after that we need to get our home study updated to indicate that we're prepared for a special-needs child. Then we'll apply to US Immigration for another child. It'll all take a month or two or three, and then we'll come back for him."

Jaden's whole body froze. He was sure he couldn't possibly be hearing correctly. He stopped crying. He was stunned. "What? Adopt Dimash?" he finally asked.

"Yes," Penni answered firmly.

Jaden began crying even harder than he had been before. He threw his arms around Penni. "Thank you, Mom. I mean . . . thank you." And, just like that, a light switched on in his head, and he knew something. For the first time, he realized he loved her. And once he realized this, he realized that he had—a little bit, at least—for a while.

"I've already called Akerke," Penni explained. "She's going to arrange it. For more money, of course. We'll have to find a way. And I need to prepare my family, to hold my head high and say to people like my sister, 'This is going to be our family dynamic, love it or leave it.'"

"I can sell my motorcycle," Steve said.

"Honey, really? Are you sure?" Penni asked.

"Yes, with no reservations—well, maybe some, but I need to do this for our family."

Jaden could have thrown his arms around Steve, but he'd never done it before, even to manipulate him, so it would have felt strange. "Thanks, Dad," he said instead. But what the heck. He hugged Steve.

It felt weird, so he started to pull away, but Steve held him tight. Finally Steve loosened his grip, and Jaden was able to pull away.

Jaden suddenly knew the reason why his biological mother had abandoned him. The reason was so that he could end up right here, right now, saving Dimash.

He couldn't sleep at first that night, just sat up and cried from the sheer hugeness of all this adoption stuff. But when he finally opened his eyes, he knew that he had fallen asleep at some point. The first thing he thought was, *Dimash is going to be my brother!* He could hear Ramazan crying and hopped out of bed to get the baby from Penni and Steve.

He knew something: He was truly this baby's brother, the same as he would be Dimash's brother. He took the baby in his arms, and they cried together. Snot dripped down his face as he cried and the baby screamed. He paced up and down the apartment, over and over and over and over, holding tightly the whole time, thinking that somehow by this holding and squeezing, their electricity was becoming enmeshed. Then, after several hours of ferocious crying, Ramazan fell asleep.

As if the silence had awakened them, Penni and Steve came into the living room. "I'll take the next shift when he wakes up," Penni said.

Jaden said simply, "I like him."

Penni asked, "You do?"

"Yeah." It was a lie, kind of. He didn't know if he truly even liked the baby yet, but he knew he'd decided that he would, someday. He would teach him whatever—how to swim, how to walk, how to build a lamp. Whatever. He knew it would be very hard, and he knew he couldn't immediately change, couldn't immediately become a kid who knew how to love. But he would try.

Acknowledgments

As always, thanks to the amazing team at Simon & Schuster. Sometimes I can't believe how lucky I am to have landed with them. My editor, Caitlyn Dlouhy, has changed my life in so many ways. Profound thanks as well to Justin Chanda, Russell Gordon, and Jeannie Ng. And thank you, thank you, thank you to my amazing agent, Gail Hochman.

I'd also like to express my deepest appreciation to adoptive moms Diane Kalkowski and Season Schultz for trusting me with their experiences and the intensity of their feelings. Thanks also to adoptive mom Karen Ballinger for reading the manuscript and giving much-needed advice, as well as sharing her blog. And thank you to adoptive moms Cindy Frogatt, Jennifer Gilbert, Kimberly Patton, Tamara Rossotti, Melissa Scott, Cathy Williams, and Shanna Wilons . . . plus any moms I've missed.

Former Peace Corps volunteers Michael Hotard and Chris Chaplin, who were both stationed in

Kazakhstan, were more than generous with their time. And thank you to falconers Steve Bodio and Lauren McGrough, and to Zena Tursynova and Zhanat Ismalova.

And, as always, thank you to my son, Sammy, who is my life and inspiration.